Pearl was willing to do whatever she could to help her husband. . .

"Your wrists are swollen!"

He touched his lips to them and her breath caught in a light gasp at the sweet, spontaneous gesture. "They . . .they're fine, truly. I just didn't realize milking was so hard."

He kept her arm in his hands as he turned his gaze to hers. The corners of his mouth tipped up. "Did I actually hear you admit there's something a man can do better than a woman? After all the times you told John and me that you could do anything we could do?"

"I didn't say a man could do it better; I only said it's hard. My muscles will become accustomed to it."

He stood, pulling her up with him. "No, they won't. You aren't to do it again."

It was the first time he'd given her an order. An order it definitely was, in spite of his tender tone.

When she opened her mouth to protest, he laid his fingers over her lips. "I spend all day in the field and around animals, until I can smell them in my sleep. I don't want my wife to smell like cows."

The gentleness in his eyes stilled any further protest. "I only meant to help. You've been so tired lately."

His hand cupped her chin lightly, his thumb tracing her cheekbone. She trembled at his touch. "You are so sweet." His husky whisper sent goose bumps down her spine. He was so close. Was he. . .was he going to kiss her?

JOANN A. GROTE made her **Heartsong Presents** debut with the historical novel, *The Sure Promise*, a story set in western Minnesota where JoAnn was raised. Grote follows that success with the sequel, *Love's Shining Hope*. Grote feels strongly that fiction has an important place in spreading God's message of salvation and encouraging Christians to become more like Christ.

Books by JoAnn A. Grote

HEARTSONG PRESENTS

HP36—The Sure Promise
HP51—The Unfolding Heart
HP55—Treasure of the Heart

Love's
Shining Hope

JoAnn A. Grote

Heartsong Presents

To

SHARON OLSEN FALVEY

My sister,

My friend.

A note from the Author:
I love to hear from my readers! You may write to me at the
following address:

JoAnn A. Grote
Author Relations
P.O. Box 719
Uhrichsville, OH 44683

ISBN 1-55748-590-9

LOVE'S SHINING HOPE

PRINTED IN THE U.S.A.

one

"Marry you, Jason?" A sophisticated little laugh cut sharply through the early August twilight. "Don't be silly."

Pearl Wells caught her breath at her best friend's condescending tone. Dismay welled up in her chest. When she'd sat down to await Miranda thirty minutes earlier, she'd never intended to eavesdrop on a lovers' quarrel!

Her spine pressed her blue Eton jacket against the high back of the wooden porch bench. If only she could get away without being seen! But the couple was too close—just around the corner where the wide porch continued its journey about the pleasant two-story clapboard building.

"Silly? We've talked of marrying since we were children!"

The shock in Jason's voice echoed that in Pearl's mind. She could imagine his usually laughing, golden brown eyes widening beneath gleaming, russet-brown hair.

"We *were* children," Miranda responded. "Until you went to school in Chicago three years ago and I went to St. Paul last fall, we never left Chippewa City. Besides," a petulant note crept into her voice, "our plans never included running your parents' farm on the Minnesota prairie and raising your brothers and sisters."

"Our plans didn't include my parents dying in a buggy accident three weeks ago, either." Jason's bitter tone burned into Pearl's heart with the searing heat of a branding iron.

"Your parents were so proud of your plans to be an architect. Surely they wouldn't expect you to throw them away."

"Are you sure that your concern is for me? You seem to have developed the popular attitude that farmers are somehow less important than townspeople. Perhaps you just don't care to be a farmer's wife." His voice could have formed ice.

Pearl pressed her hands firmly over her ears. She wouldn't listen to any more of this private conversation! But her small hands couldn't shut out the embarrassing scene.

"You've always known I don't want to live on a farm. A farmer's wife has a hard life. I won't grow old before my time working my fingers to the bone when instead I can live as a lady is meant to live."

"You mean with less deserving women performing your household chores?"

"You needn't sound so scornful. As an architect, you'll have a much different life as an adult than you did as a child. With your talent and personality, you are certain to be a success. Naturally your wife will be busy with social obligations."

"Sounds as though it's the architect you love rather than the man." Jason's low, sharp words almost didn't make it through the barrier Pearl had tried to erect. She wished fervently they hadn't.

Exasperation filled Miranda's sigh. "I simply want what is best for you."

"Trust me to know what that is. I'm asking you again to marry me. I give you fair warning that my plans to be an architect are behind me. I can't foresee a time I'll be leaving the farm or my family."

"Then my answer must be no."

A huge, burning rock seemed to replace Pearl's heart. How could Miranda say no?

"My answer will be yes when you give up this preposterous idea—"

"I'll not give it up. If you think so little of me that you believe I could walk away from my family when they need me, perhaps it's best that you refuse me."

A dog howled in the distance and was answered by another. Jason's horse snorted, and another horse's hooves plodded down a nearby street. The slight sweet scent of the bushes in front of the porch railing drifted on the barely moving air. Pearl held her breath, waiting for the silence to end between the two who had loved each other for so many years. Her fingers slipped from their ineffectual place over her ears. She lowered them slowly to the wide arms of the bench, inadvertently brushing her jacket's leghorn sleeve against something on the small table beside her.

Too late, she realized she had knocked over a porcelain pot of geraniums. She grasped for it as it fell and watched in horror as it crashed to pieces on the painted wooden floor.

Silence followed. Pearl closed her eyes tight and took a deep breath before standing up. There'd be no more hiding from Jason and Miranda.

"Who's there?"

Jason's bark was more of a demand than a question, Pearl thought, lifting her tailored blue serge skirt and stepping around the dirt, blossoms, and broken porcelain. She stopped short around the corner, just past the darkest shadows.

The couple stood in the yellow rectangle made by the sitting room lamp shining through the window. Jason was standing as straight and tall as ever, his shoulders broad beneath his long roll gray suit, black crepe wrapped around the crown of his derby in traditional mourning manner.

"It's only me. I was waiting for Miranda."

"So you could eavesdrop on us?"

Anger fired through her at Jason's suspicion. It was embarrassing enough to be in this situation without being accused of having staged it. "Naturally, I could think of nothing more exciting to do with my evening than listen to the two of you quarrel!"

She regretted her sarcasm immediately. Jason's emotions must be raw from Miranda's treatment. It wasn't like him to attack her so crudely. She gripped her hands together behind her and forced her voice to a softer and lower level. "I apologize to you both. I truly didn't intend to eavesdrop. It's just that you were suddenly here, and quarreling, and there didn't seem to be a path of escape."

"It's all right, Pearl," Miranda pardoned her carelessly.

Pearl didn't care whether Miranda forgave her after the way she'd treated Jason. She glanced at him. He'd never been a handsome man, but definitely appealing with his ready grin and laughing eyes—eyes that could be so warm and steady. They reminded her of the sun the first time she looked into them across a sheet of gray ice the day he'd saved her life.

There was nothing warm about his eyes tonight.

"I guess you would have heard about it anyway. You and Miranda tell each other everything." Jason didn't sound as though he was forgiving her. Would he ever look at her without remembering that she'd heard Miranda refuse his proposal? If she lost his friendship.... A shudder went through her at the thought.

Jason turned away from her. "Good-bye, Miranda."

The pain that throbbed in the short farewell brought instant tears to sting against Pearl's eyelids. She bit hard into her lips to keep from crying out as he crossed the porch, each step an exclamation point against the narrow wooden boards.

Pearl remained frozen until the buggy disappeared, then turned to Miranda. She was standing at the top of the steps with one black lace glove against a white wooden pillar. Her thick, dark hair was piled high above her slightly round face beneath one of the hats she loved. A firefly flared and faded against the black silk gown she wore in sympathy with Jason's grieving.

"I cannot believe you refused him."

"When he's thought it over, he'll realize I'm right, and he'll come back."

Pearl doubted it. She'd known Jason as long as Miranda had known him. He wouldn't be Jason Sterling if he left his family for her. "You mean when he realizes you're right about leaving his family to their own devices?"

Miranda settled gracefully into a white wooden rocker in front of the sitting room window. "You make it sound vile. With his fine, quick mind and talented fingers, Jason would be miserable as a farmer."

"He shall be miserable if he doesn't care for his family. Don't you know the man at all?"

The small glow of lamplight touched Miranda's lips in their condescending smile. "It may hurt him now, but eventually he'll realize that he has to pursue his career as an architect, has to live the life he was created to live. When that happens, you and Jason will both see that love for him is behind my refusal to marry him now."

Pearl shook her head slowly. "I shall never believe love behaves in such a manner —forcing the person one claims to love to abandon his principles. You should be proud that the man who loves you is God-fearing, unselfish, and fine."

Miranda's superior laugh rang through the evening air. "You've been reading too many romantic serials. Sacrifice seems noble in a story, but in true life, it is only painful and hard. Jason has always known what he wanted to do with his life, and it isn't farming."

"You always knew what you wanted to do with your life, also. You wanted to be Jason's wife."

"Only after the manner we've planned, especially after the time I've spent in St. Paul. I met fascinating people there, had entrance to elegant homes, was escorted to fine eating establishments, wore beautiful gowns."

"Are you certain you haven't fallen in love with one of your city-bred escorts?" Pearl was almost ashamed of her question. When Miranda wrote of the men she was seeing while in St. Paul, Pearl had been horrified that she would treat her commitment to Jason so lightly. Miranda had insisted that her escorts were merely friends, and Pearl's loyalty had been quick to accept her explanation. Now, she wondered anew.

Miranda's gaze dropped to her lap, where her lace-covered fingers played with her fine silk skirt. "I could hardly go about the city unescorted. Aunt Elsie was kind enough to insist I experience the benefits of culture the city provided, and arranged for her friends' sons to accompany me."

"They must have been weak examples of manhood that you no longer recognize the worth of a man like Jason."

"I won't apologize for liking life as I experienced it there. Jason and I can have a similar life. I don't intend to allow him to give it away in a moment of sentimental self-sacrifice."

Pearl took an impulsive step nearer, her hands balling into fists at her sides. "Sentimental! I do believe Jason's right. You aren't thinking of him at all. You're thinking of yourself, and a life filled with empty grasping instead of giving! Why, I can hardly believe you're the same sweet, innocent girl with whom I grew up!"

The rocker stopped short as Miranda's back stiffened. "I'm not that girl. I've become a woman during the year in St. Paul, and I'm not a whit ashamed of that woman."

"I spent months advancing my music training at the Northwestern Conservatory of Music in Minneapolis, but I hope I haven't become as self-seeking and superior as you've grown. Jason's life is disintegrating around him. He's lost his parents and given up his career, and now he's lost you, too."

"He hasn't lost me. I told you, he'll be back."

Pearl shook her head so hard that some of her blond curls came unpinned and slid down her neck. "Not if he has to meet your demands. He has too much honor. How *could* you hurt him so unbearably when he needs your love and understanding now more than ever?"

A high little laugh escaped Miranda's heart-shaped lips and her eyes widened in surprise. "Why, I do believe you are in love with Jason yourself!"

Pearl flushed. After all these years, had she given away her secret in a moment of anger? Although she and Jason were good friends, it was Miranda who had caught his heart. Never had she revealed her love to anyone, and now. . . . It wouldn't do for Miranda to know of it now, when she'd become a stranger and treated Jason's love so lightly. "You're only attempting to change the subject because you know you cannot defend the way you've treated him."

Miranda shot out of the chair and stood quaking only inches away from Pearl. "What gives you the right to judge me, or to tell me how to deal with my fiancé?"

"The right of one who has been a friend to both of you since we were ten years old. And he's not your fiancé. You ended that tonight when you threw his love back in his face."

Miranda's hand streaked out to land a resounding slap on Pearl's cheek.

Pearl gasped, blinking against the sting of the unexpected blow. Turning sharply on her high-heeled, high-buttoned shoes, she grasped her slender skirt and hurried down the steps and away from the friend she'd loved like a sister.

The burning in her cheek seemed minor compared to the fire in her chest. *To think anyone would treat Jason's love in such a trifling manner!* He must be aching horribly over Miranda's refusal. One would think his love would die a sudden and merciful death upon realizing that the woman he cared for was selfish and wholly unworthy of that love. At eighteen, she wasn't so young and inexperienced as to believe love died so easily.

If it did, her own love for Jason would have died years ago when she discovered he was madly in love with her best friend. Instead it took root all the more fiercely and grew taller and stronger than an oak beside a river. She'd tried to care for other men, but every potential suitor had paled beside Jason Sterling. If he had asked *her* to marry him, she'd have accepted so quickly it would have set his head spinning.

two

Pearl closed the door behind her last piano student and hurried to the shed to harness her horse, Angel, to her stepfather's buggy. Large baskets of bread and apple pies she'd baked the night before were placed on the floor and seat, covered with towels to protect them from flies and the dust of the road.

Her conscience had been prickling for a day and a half—ever since that night on Miranda's porch. When Jason's parents died, she'd attended the funeral with her stepparents, Dr. Matthew Strong and his wife, whom Pearl had always called Mother Boston. She'd expressed her condolences, and Mother Boston had sent out a basket of food. Of course, she'd been praying for Jason and his family, but she was ashamed to admit she hadn't realized they might need more substantial assistance.

She wasn't certain of what that assistance might consist. However, since the oldest woman in the home was now Maggie, Jason's twelve-year-old sister, she was sure baked goods would be appreciated.

Fields began almost before she left the prairie town. The hay crops were mostly garnered, and hay stacks dotted the fields, along with men and horses beginning to harvest barley and early wheat. The heady smell of the ripe grains filled the air. She loved the way friendly clouds sent lilac shadows weaving over the golden fields.

The buggy's red wheels settled into the well-worn ruts in the dirt road, their rattle bringing curious prairie dogs from their holes. The plop, plop of Angel's hooves and the swish of the wind through the fields kept up a constant background to Pearl's thoughts.

She and her brother, Johnny, had lived with their stepparents since she was two and he was six. Although Dr. Matt and Mother Boston had surrounded them with all the love two children could ask, she and Johnny had maintained a special bond through the years.

Jason and Johnny had been good friends from the time Jason's family moved into the area eight years earlier. Perhaps it was Johnny's attitude that caused Jason to be so accepting toward her. She was so comfortable with him! He was like a second brother.

A yellow-breasted meadowlark lit on a weed-top and trilled its song as Pearl turned off onto the lane leading to Jason's farmstead. The two-story white clapboard house was dwarfed by the red barn, the machine shed, and corncribs. She recalled Jason speaking of the house being built in the eighties. Those had been profitable years for the farmers, and fine farm homes had replaced most of the sod huts and small homes that were common in the seventies.

Cottonwoods and maples had been planted around the house and beside the lane years ago, but they were still young. She smiled at the sound of the thick, shiny cottonwood leaves clapping in the wind, as if applauding her decision to come.

Smells of animal life assailed her, drawing her attention to the brown and white cows gazing idly at her over the fence and to the hogs lazily grunting in another fenced section near the farm building most distant from the house. She knew Jason's father had kept only a few cows and hogs to meet the family's needs, and considered the crops his livelihood, though dairy farming was the primary means of support for most area farmers.

As she tied Angel to the white fence enclosing the yard, she noticed the weed-infested garden off to one side, near the fields. The pansies lifting their cheery heads beside the porch, however, grew weed free, and she wondered at the inconsistency.

It was Maggie who responded to her knock on the kitchen screen door, her broad face pale and plain between two long brown braids. The girl's suspiciously red eyes opened wide at the sight of the piano teacher. "Miss Wells!"

Pearl politely ignored the signs of her grief and smiled cheerfully. "Hello. I over-baked and decided to share my bounty."

"How kind! Won't you come in?" Maggie held the screen door while Pearl entered the large square kitchen and placed the baskets on the rectangular oak table in the middle of the room.

Pearl had never been inside Jason's home and she glanced eagerly about the high-ceilinged kitchen. There were windows on two walls, filling the room with late summer sunlight. The wainscoting was shiny white, and the walls above it a cheerful yellow. The furnishings were surprisingly up-to-date. Pale blue curtains fluttered at the open, screened windows.

It warmed her heart that Jason's mother had tried to make the workroom of the house such a welcoming place for the family. True, table, work table, sink and all other available space was filled with dirty dishes and failed baking attempts, but that only went to prove that she was justified in coming out here. "What a cheerful room!"

The pain in Maggie's white face brought her up short. She'd assumed the girl's red eyes were due to grieving over her parents. Now she saw that Maggie was cradling one arm carefully with her other.

Pearl winced at the long burn on the inside of the forearm, beneath a rolled-up sleeve. "From the stove?"

Maggie nodded, her teeth hard in her bottom lip.

Pearl retrieved a chipped graniteware bowl and pitcher from

the back porch and placed cold, wet cloths on the wound and on the girl's forehead. Inside the small oak refrigerator, she found butter, and under Maggie's guidance located a clean cloth in the pantry. Dirty clothes overflowed a wicker basket onto the pantry floor, making it difficult to walk in the small room.

"I was baking bread," Maggie explained while Pearl spread the wound with butter and wrapped it. With a feeble wave of her hand, she indicated an exceedingly flat loaf sitting on a square of wooden slats on the work table. She sighed and slumped against the straight chair back. "I was hoping to have some bread and pie ready for when the neighbors and hired men help with the harvesting in a couple days. Today seemed like a good time, since my brothers are helping in Thor Lindstrom's fields—he's our neighbor—and there were only five-year-old Grace and me to make dinner for."

Was Maggie trying to run the household all by herself? Pearl tried to hide how the thought horrified her. "Don't you have a hired girl to help?"

Maggie's shaggy brown braids wiggled as she shook her head. "She married in December and Jason hasn't found anyone to replace her." She rubbed a hand self-consciously over the dirty apron covering her wrinkled green-and-white dress. "I can't seem to keep up with everything around the house like Mom did. Baking is the worst. I'm pretty hopeless at it."

Pearl patted the younger girl's shoulder briskly. "No one is hopeless. I'll teach you to make wonderful bread." There were some things she planned to teach Jason, too, about expecting a girl to take over a woman's responsibilities.

Maggie looked up at her eagerly. "Do you really think I could learn? Frank and Andy make fun of my baking and cooking. Frank even brought home bread from Carl's Bakery last time he was in town. Jason tells them to quit teasing me, but even he doesn't clean his plate the way he did when Mom cooked."

"We'll show Frank and Andrew what a woman can do in a kitchen. In fact, I intend to stay the rest of the day and help you catch up on your housework a bit." She held an index finger up in a prim, piano-instructor manner as Maggie opened her mouth to object. "It's simply the neighborly thing to do, and I won't be put off."

A frown crinkled the girl's brow, and she rolled her hands in her dirty apron. "Jason may not like it if you help. He says it's my place to take care of the house now that Mom's gone."

"I'll see to Jason. Now, if you'll lend me an apron, we'll get busy with this kitchen." Pearl pulled the pins from her flower-covered straw hat. Hoping to cheer Maggie, she said, "Your flower bed looks nice."

Maggie's eyes clouded over again. "Jason weeded the flowers by lantern last night. He said he didn't want Mom's flowers to die." The hint of a sob caught in her sigh. "I can't seem to do everything he wants me to."

"I'm sure Jason thought no such thing when he tended to the flowers. It was only a way to comfort himself by doing something he thought your mother would like."

Hope relieved some of the tense lines in Maggie's face, but she said nothing.

The afternoon wasn't nearly long enough to accomplish all that needed to be done. The kitchen was hot from the growing heat of the early August day, and from the large cookstove that stood along the wall between the kitchen and the dining room—the better to offer heat to more of the home during the winter months. They used water heated in the reservoir at the back of the stove during Maggie's baking attempts to wash the myriad of dirty dishes and to scrub the floor.

Pearl was frying chicken for supper when Grace called

excitedly from the post she'd taken up for the last thirty minutes beside one of the kitchen windows. "The boys are
comin'!" She was out the door in a flash, racing to greet the
men, her shoulder-length dark brown hair flying.

Pearl's heart leaped to her throat. Jason! He'd be inside
any minute now. She wiped perspiration from her forehead
with the back of a hand which still held the large fork she was
using to turn the chicken and she moaned slightly in dismay.
She must look a wreck! Stray bits of her hair were curling
wetly against her forehead and cheeks. Her trim chambray
dress of tiny blue plaid with a plaited front—chosen to compliment her eyes—was no longer crisply fresh.

Through the nearest window she saw Jason stop beside her
buggy. He scooped Grace up in his arms and her giggle floated
through the open window as Pearl turned back to the stove.
Children always loved Jason, with his open, fun-loving manner. She envied Grace. She'd like to greet him so freely
herself!

The men's responses to Grace's chatter mixed with the
splashing of water as they washed up on the porch. The door
slammed and Frank's voice moved ahead of his heavy boots
as he crossed the kitchen to stare over Pearl's shoulder. In
spite of his recent washing, he smelled of earth and grain and
the kerosene farmers used to discourage flies and mosqui-
toes.

"Pearl Wells, as I live and breathe, frying chicken on our
cookstove. Are you real or is this a dream?"

A laugh bubbled forth at the usually reserved Frank's teasing. They were the same age, and the two of them were quite
good friends. With his black hair, thin black mustache and normally somber dark eyes, he was handsome and brooding in a
manner that won girls' sympathetic hearts easily, but it was
Jason's laughing, golden brown eyes she preferred. At least,
they used to laugh most of the time, before his parents died.

"I'm definitely not a dream—assuming you were referring to me and not the chicken."

"Of course I was referring to you!" His eyes opened innocently wide. "Though I'm glad to see you're accompanied by the chicken."

"Me, too!" thirteen-year-old Andrew piped up from the other side of her. His face was a duplicate of Maggie's beneath straight, light brown hair. "We haven't had a decent meal around here in days."

"Thanks a bunch, Andy!" Maggie pushed him aside indignantly and held out a large platter for Pearl to place the chicken on.

"Neither of you shall have any supper until you've removed your boots. You should be ashamed of yourselves, walking over Maggie's clean floor in those filthy things."

Out of the corner of her eye, she saw Jason beside the door. She stifled a laugh at the sight of him guiltily removing his boots beside his chastened brothers.

Maggie pulled fresh rolls from the oven and took corn-on-the-cob from the stove while Pearl made the gravy. When the food was on the table and everyone was standing impatiently behind their chairs waiting to sit down, she realized Jason was still standing at the door. He was staring at her grimly.

She smiled at him in spite of the lead ball that hit her stomach at the growl in his eyes. "Well, Mr. Head-of-the-house, aren't you going to join us?"

The veins stood out like cords on the darkly-tanned forearms crossed over his sweaty work shirt. His voice was quiet and polite, but that didn't deceive her after the thunderclouds she saw in his eyes. "What are you doing here?"

"Who cares? Look at this feast!"

"I wasn't speaking to you, Andy." Jason's gaze didn't flicker from Pearl's face.

"She's just helping me, Jason. Don't be angry."

"I wasn't speaking to you, either, Maggie."

"I just stopped by with some extra baked goods, and. . ."

"'Just stopped by' three miles from your house?"

"And decided to stay for dinner. Which is getting cold, by the way."

They stared at each other, and Pearl wondered nervously what he would say next. Didn't he realize he was making everyone uncomfortable? This wasn't anything like the Jason she'd known so many years.

Her hands closed tightly around the top of the chair in front of her. "Well, I guess the way to your heart isn't through your stomach."

Frank and Andy guffawed, and even Maggie laughed. Pearl thought she saw a slight softening in the set of Jason's mouth, but decided a moment later that she'd never been more mistaken in her life.

His words lashed at her. "You have no right to come into my home and take over like this."

three

Pearl swallowed her shock. She'd expected Jason to be uncomfortable with her after she'd witnessed Miranda refuse his proposal, but she hadn't expected him to react so rudely in front of his family.

"Jason!"

Frank's sharp bark of disapproval jerked Jason's gaze from hers, and he had the decency to flush hotly beneath his tan.

"I apologize," he muttered, his stance making it obvious that the words were a social requirement only.

She hoped no one noticed her lips trembling beneath her smile. "Won't you sit down to supper? We can continue this discussion later, if you wish."

One corner of his mouth lifted in the suspicion of a smile. "Well, it does smell mighty good."

Beside her, Maggie echoed Pearl's small sigh of relief as Jason pulled out a chair at the head of the table and slipped into it. The rest of the family quickly followed suit, and Pearl heard Andrew mutter a low "About time!" Following a brief prayer, the food was quickly passed around, and silence ensued as everyone began eating.

Evidently the silence was too much for Grace to bear. She held a greasy drumstick in one hand, looked everyone over calmly with large, chocolate brown eyes beneath hair that touched her eyebrows. "Maggie burned her arm t'day."

Everyone stopped eating and stared first at Grace and then at Maggie. Grace grinned with gratification at the disturbance her announcement caused and promptly began eating.

"Maggie?" Jason's forehead furrowed into a frown.

Maggie fidgeted slightly and looked down at her plate. "It's not too bad, honest." She slipped her arm to her lap.

The girl's fear and dread of Jason was disturbing to Pearl. Didn't Maggie understand that it wasn't her that made Jason angry, but the pain of losing their parents?

"May I see it?"

At Jason's gruff request, Maggie held out her bandaged forearm. "Miss Wells looked after it for me."

"Maggie cwied," Grace announced with satisfaction, and Maggie scowled at her.

Jason gently unwrapped the bandage. Maggie gave a little gasp and dug her teeth into her bottom lip. His gaze darted to her face, then he peeked under the loosened end of the covering. His eyelids slammed shut.

"How did it happen?"

Maggie answered his tight question as he carefully retied the covering. "Burned it on the stove. I should have been more careful."

Jason leaned over to kiss her forehead. "I'm sorry, Sweetie."

The guilt in his voice and face both hurt and comforted Pearl. His actions were much more in keeping with the Jason she'd always known than the stern man that frightened Maggie so terribly.

When the pie had been devoured among numerous and extreme compliments, Pearl rose and began to clear the table.

"Maggie will clean up." Jason's tone let it be known his decision was final.

"Her injured arm won't be able to endure the hot dishwater." Pearl tried to state the fact without sounding defensive.

"Then Andy can wash the dishes."

"Aw, Jase, that's women's work!"

"It needs doing, Andy. Maggie can wipe them for you."

"I don't mind helping Maggie," Pearl protested.

"I'm going to hitch up your horse and take you home. It's

already late and I have to be in the fields early."

"I don't need an escort."

He reached for the sweaty beige hat he'd hung on the peg behind the door. Settling it on his head, he turned to look at her. "No lady is leaving my home in the dark without an escort."

He left the house without waiting for her reply. *Wonderful,* she thought. *Now I'm feeling guilty for keeping him out late when he obviously isn't getting all the sleep he needs as it is!*

They'd traveled half a mile through the grain- and earth-scented night before she gave up hoping he would end the silence between them, and spoke herself.

"You needn't act like such an ogre. I was only helping."

"I don't need your pity." His tone was harder than the rocks the wheels hit in the road. "You don't have to play nursemaid to me because Miranda turned me down."

"You. . .you. . .oh!" Pearl could hardly stop sputtering. "You think I pity you because of Miranda? On the contrary, I think you were fortunate to get out of her clutches!"

"Fortunate?" He drew hard on the lines, drawing Angel to an abrupt halt that set the carriage rocking precariously and brought a nervous whinny from his own horse, tied behind. Jason's eyes blazed in the light that darted over his face from the swinging lanterns. "You think I'm *fortunate* to lose her?"

"Yes! No. I don't know." Her arms clenched tightly over her chest. He wouldn't appreciate hearing how her heart went out to him when Miranda turned him down.

Her voice was only a throaty whisper the prairie night tried to snatch away. "I think we both lost her. I miss her, too."

After her quarrel with Miranda, she'd felt so empty. Now it appeared she was losing Jason's friendship, also.

"I don't understand."

It was the friendliest his tone had been toward her all

evening. Relief loosened the tightness in her chest. "I. . .I as much as told her she was a fool not to marry you."

"I don't know whether to thank you or upbraid you."

"I know it wasn't my affair, but. . . ."

"But that's never stopped you before." The tremor of a laugh jiggled his words.

"You and Miranda are my best friends! If I can't be honest with you, with whom can I be?"

"I assume she wasn't pleased with your interference?"

"No." *Interference!* That put her in her place. "How could a year in St. Paul have changed Miranda so?"

"I don't know." Hopelessness filled his voice.

The plopping of horses' hooves, the swish of Angel's tail, the singing of crickets, and the thumping of moths against the lanterns all sounded incredibly loud in the night air. Pearl longed to reach out to Jason, to let him know that he wasn't alone or unloved because one woman had been fool enough to let him out of her life.

"You've never been to the farm before, so why now, two days after Miranda. . ." She heard him swallow hard. "If it's not out of pity, why come now?"

"I only meant to leave some baked goods. But when Maggie told me how she was trying to take your mother's place—and failing miserably—and I saw how much needed to be done, and worst of all how afraid she is of you. . . ."

Jason swung to face her, his square jaw dropping. "Afraid?"

"Yes. She didn't say it in so many words, but she's terrified of displeasing you."

He snorted. "That's ridiculous."

"You've given her an adult's responsibilities before she's even through grieving for her parents. She isn't prepared for those duties."

"Someone has to take care of the cooking and laundry and such."

"Naturally. But a twelve-year-old?"

"There isn't anyone else. What do you expect me to do? Give up working in the fields or caring for the livestock? Give up sleeping to do the household chores?"

Pearl gritted her teeth and swallowed the anger that rose in her throat at his sarcasm. He was impossible! Had she expected him to remain the easygoing boy with the constant grin and laughing eyes she'd always known, she reprimanded herself. Did she think a person could lose his parents, his fiancée's love and support, and the work he loved without being affected by his loss?

She took a deep breath and counted to ten, gripping her patience to keep her voice calm. "Maggie said you've already tried unsuccessfully to hire help. Until you can find someone, you might accept the help of friends."

Jason stared stonily ahead a moment longer, then brushed his floppy hat back further on his head and wiped a hand down his face with a weariness that caught at Pearl's heart anew. "My family isn't your responsibility."

"We're friends. That makes us each other's responsibility."

He grabbed her arm, and she was forced to look into the eyes only inches from her own, eyes that looked stormy in the swaying lantern light. "Can't you understand? When the grieving time is over, there's still going to be the fieldwork and the animals to care for and the garden and the housework. That isn't going to change. So *we* have to change— me and Frank and Andy and Maggie and even Grace. We have to learn to rely on ourselves."

A chill swept through her at the raw pain in his fierce explanation. He was right; she hadn't understood.

He dropped her arm with a muttered apology.

It took a few minutes for Pearl to regain her courage, for she had no intention of letting the matter drop. "I understand now why you're so angry about my helping out. Just the same, Maggie is too young. . ." She held up a hand as if to ward him off as he turned toward her. "Let me finish! Maggie is too young and inexperienced to take on all your mother's responsibilities yet. If I. . .that is, if you *let* me. . .help out for a bit, I can teach her some of the things your mother hadn't time to teach her."

He took so long to respond that she almost thought he wouldn't answer. When he did, there was no anger left in his voice, only regret. "Is she really frightened of me?"

Impulsively, she laid a hand on his arm. "She's only afraid of disappointing you, not that you'll punish her."

"When I saw that burn, I felt so guilty." His groan seemed to echo through her chest. "I'd never realized the things that could happen to her and Grace while we're out in the fields."

"They could happen even if you're home."

He looked up at the expanse of dark blue above them, where a handful of stars were beginning to peek through. "It seems the last few weeks I can't leave anyone I care about for even a few minutes without wondering whether I'll ever see them alive again."

"I'm sure that's only natural." She wished there were something more soothing to say.

"If it's been hard for me, it must be more difficult for my brothers and sisters, being younger. How could Miranda think I would cause them additional pain by leaving them now?"

Would his heart never heal from Miranda's betrayal?

"Do you agree with her, Pearl?"

Her head snapped up. "No! Of course not. Your family needs you."

A sigh whooshed out of him. "That's what I believe, too."

"Jason," she started cautiously, "what if you sold the farm? Could you care for the family in town on what you can earn as an architect?"

"Farms are going dirt cheap with the hard times the country's experiencing. If we could sell it, we'd barely make enough to pay off Dad's bank notes. Then, too, I'd like to keep the farm in case Frank or Andy wants it one day. Besides, I was only beginning as an architect—haven't proven myself yet. Certainly couldn't guarantee making enough to support five people."

"I only thought if there was a way you could stay in architecture and live in town, perhaps Miranda. . . ."

"She objected to my family as well as my vocation." From the tautness in his voice, she knew this had hurt him more than anything else in Miranda's rejection.

He reached for her hand, squeezing her fingers so tightly she had to clamp her lips together hard to keep from crying out. "You're a good friend, always have been. I'm afraid I took advantage of that friendship tonight and let a lot of the anger and frustration that's built up in me the last few weeks tumble out on you. I'm sorry."

The niggling fear that their friendship had been lost in the recent happenings released. Her eyelids pressed tightly closed as she lifted a quick prayer of thanksgiving heavenward. "Our friendship is strong enough to withstand some onslaughts. You've forgiven a few faults in me over the years."

Lantern light revealed the tender smile in Jason's eyes as he squeezed her hand once more, not so hard this time.

The matter of her helping out on the farm hadn't been settled, and when they'd entered Chippewa City and were nearing her stepparents' home, she broached the subject again.

"I promised Maggie I'd help with the laundry in the morning." She hoped her tone said this was as natural as the sun rising.

His chuckle was a relief. "Sometimes you're so stubborn you make a Missouri mule look downright amiable by comparison. Guess I knew I was beaten before we even began discussing the matter."

She wished she'd known it!

"But I'll only agree to your helping until you've taught Maggie a few things," he continued before she had time to savor her victory.

"Yes, sir," she replied meekly, not about to let him know how her heart was racing with joy and anticipation.

He laughed outright this time. Pulling up in front of her house, he bounced a broad, callused index finger off the tip of her nose. "I can see I'm in trouble now. You never act so humble without some mischief up your sleeve."

She grinned from the sheer joy of seeing laughter back in his eyes once more.

His arm slipped around her shoulder, giving her a brief hug. "Thanks for standing by me, friend," he said in a low, gruff voice. It was all she could do to keep from throwing her arms about his neck and telling him she would always stand by him.

Over Pearl's protests, Jason unhooked Angel and took her to the shed behind the house to brush, feed, and water while Pearl went inside and lit a lamp.

Looking down from the saddle when he was ready to leave, he grinned at her. "That apple pie sure hit the spot tonight. Think you could teach Maggie how to make that, right off?"

Without waiting for a reply, he turned his mount and started out of town. Pearl could hardly believe her ears when a whistled tune floated back to her. When she could no longer see his shadow or hear his whistle, she tilted her head back to take in the stars twinkling in the dark blue bowl of the sky.

"Thank you, Lord, for beginning to heal him."

four

Jason Sterling leaned against a wooden support on the porch, hands stuffed into the back pockets of his jeans, and watched the rain pouring over the fields. It was coming down good and steady, but not hard enough to damage the unharvested crops. If he was as good at reading the weather as he thought, they wouldn't be out of the fields more than a day or two.

He was almost glad for the reprieve. The harvester needed repairing. So did his muscles. He lifted his shoulders, then rolled them back in a stretch, wincing. He'd grown soft the last couple years, at school and working in town.

The wheat was good and plump. Harvest was going full blast. The hay crop was already mostly garnered and barley reaped. His father would have been more than satisfied with him and his brothers. Still, he thought, you could never count your money until the crop was completely harvested. Nature might have a surprise or two up her sleeve yet.

Through the open windows, Pearl's clear voice floated out to him in a sweet hymn accompanied by the parlor piano. The tension melted from his body as she sang. She'd been helping out for two weeks now, and he'd often heard her singing as she worked.

He was glad he'd agreed to her coming out to help them. She'd been good for everyone. His chuckle blended with the patter of the rain and with Pearl's clear voice. *Agreed* to her coming! It would be easier to stop a tornado than to stop Pearl once she'd set her mind on something.

She'd always been that way. Once her brother, John, had tried to patiently convince her that girls did not go fishing. It had been impossible to persuade her, even when he and John had insisted she find her own nightcrawlers and learn to bait her own hook. The relish with which she had chased down the 'crawlers amused them. She hadn't liked putting the worms on hooks, but she'd set her small pink lips in a determined line and done it anyway. John had told him early in their friendship that their parents were gone. Jason had admired the way John looked out for Pearl and the two boys had formed an unspoken pact to always keep her under their wings. He wasn't sure she still needed their protection.

Beat all how a girl who looked so sweet and fragile could be so tough underneath. He'd learned the fact years ago. It still amused him when one of the young men in town was deceived by her femininity. To look at her, she was all frills and lace and golden curls, yet in a difficult place, he'd as soon have her on his side as a band of hardened cowboys.

His smile died. Well, he was in a difficult place now, and she was right here helping out as he should have expected. He detested himself for wishing it was Miranda instead.

It's not the real Miranda I want beside me. Surprise ripped through him at the thought. It was true. The woman he wanted was the woman he'd believed Miranda to be, not the woman she'd actually become.

With a weary sigh that came from the very tips of his mud-covered boots, he pushed himself away from the wooden support. He couldn't afford to waste his energy in self-pity. A woman who wouldn't stand by the man she loved wasn't worth all that regret anyway.

He tugged off his boots at the kitchen door and crossed the room to the parlor. Apple butter bubbling on the back of the stove made his mouth water. It was only the second year the apple trees which had been planted in the eighties had born fruit. His mother had been so proud of those apples last year.

Leaning against the door frame, he slipped his thumbs

beneath the suspenders at his waist. It was Maggie playing the piano, studiously concentrating on the pages in front of her. Grace was asleep on the plush forest-green sofa which matched the tasseled draperies, one arm curled around her doll and the other thrown out in abandonment. Pearl was in his mother's high-backed, upholstered spring rocker beneath the large hanging lamp with the rose-colored glass shade, mending one of his socks as she sang softly to Maggie's accompaniment. The homey scene eased the familiar tightness in his chest caused by thoughts of Miranda.

His mother had loved this room. He could still hear his father telling him that a farmer's wife had a hard life and deserved whatever beauty a husband could give her in return. The up-to-date furnishings had cost his father plenty, but he'd never complained. Between the modern home and conveniences and the farm implements purchased during the affluent eighties, the bank held a good-sized note for Jason and his brothers to work off.

"Sounds good, Maggie," he encouraged when the song ended. "But don't you think you should be helping Pearl with the mending?"

Maggie flushed and stood quickly, setting the round top of the piano stool in a spin.

"I asked her to play. The music relaxes me." Pearl's gaze met his, her blue eyes challenging although her tone was friendly.

Maggie bent over the never-empty tapestry mending basket beside Pearl's rocker. "I'm almost through with mending for the afternoon," Pearl told her cheerily. "Perhaps you'd check the pantry to see whether there's any of your mother's wonderful rhubarb sauce to have with the pound cake you made for supper."

"Yes, ma'am." Maggie smiled. The smile disappeared as she edged past Jason with her eyes averted, and the change twisted something sharply inside him.

"Maggie!" She stopped at his call, turning around slowly, apprehension filling her face. Was she always going to be afraid of him, he wondered in frustration? "You play well. Rev. Conrad will be asking you to play for church services soon."

The grin she flashed him was his reward.

He settled into the overstuffed chair opposite Pearl, his head resting wearily against the lace tidy. Remembering his sweaty work clothes, he dropped to the hassock near the rocker instead. Even though his mother had insisted on using the parlor for the family sitting room, she never allowed them on the furniture in their field clothes.

Elbows propped against his knees, he plowed his hands through his hair. "Did it again, didn't I? Frightened Maggie. Thought things between us were almost back to normal."

Pearl glanced up from her mending. "Remember how fragile one's pride is at that age? Besides, your compliment went a long way toward healing any bruises your earlier words may have caused."

He rubbed a hand across his jaw. "Don't know how parents manage to discipline their children without losing their love altogether. I sure haven't mastered the art."

"You've only been a parent for six weeks, and Maggie's been a child for twelve years. You're doing fine, Jason."

He studied the pattern of the Brussels carpet. "You were right about us needing you. We were all so wrapped up in our grief that we didn't know how to smile or help each other anymore. You respected our loss, but brought back some of the warmth the house had when Mom and Dad were with us." He cleared his throat, thick from emotion. She glanced up at the oil painting of his parents over the settee. "I was admiring this painting of them earlier. I'm so glad you have it to remember them by. Johnny has a small picture of my

parents on their wedding day. Sometimes I stare at their like-
nesses, trying to remember what they were like, how they
spoke, how they moved. I never succeed."

Her lips trembled before she caught her bottom lip between
her teeth and the sight caught at his heart. He slipped a hand
over one of hers. How could he have been so incredibly self-
centered? He could kick himself for being so stupid. "I'd
forgotten that you lost your parents when you were two. Being here—it must bring back a lot of painful memories."

"It's not the same as your loss. Only Mother died then.
Father just left us."

He felt as well as heard the slight sigh that escaped her and
his stomach clenched at the thought of the pain she'd gone
through as a child. It was impossible for him to understand a
man abandoning his children, even if he believed it would be
better for the children without him, as Pearl's father had
believed.

She turned toward him with a bright little smile and her
brave cheerfulness made his voice gruff. "You make me realize how blessed we've been to have our parents with us all
these years. Been pretty wrapped up in self-pity, I guess."

Her soft fingers squeezed his where they still rested over
her hands and mending. "It's only natural to grieve for what
might have been."

At her nearness and gentle sympathy, he had a sudden urge
to draw her into his arms to seek comfort for his recent losses
and to comfort her for old losses. In all the years of their
friendship, he'd never experienced such a longing, and the
intensity of it pushed all thought of conversation from his
mind as he stared at her in wonder.

Footsteps galloping down the stairway broke the silence.
Frank burst into the room, stopping short at the sight of them.
He brushed back the lock of his black hair that always in-
sisted on dropping over the middle of his forehead and grinned

at his older brother. "Forgot to tell you the big news I heard the other night at the Grange meeting. Chippewa City is going to build a combination town hall and opera hall next spring. Thought you might want to submit plans for the building."

Jason's chest felt like a bull had stomped on it. "No."

"It's a great opportunity to show the town what you can do," Frank urged.

"I can't be a successful architect and run a farm at the same time." Wouldn't he love to try to design that building! Sometimes his fingers positively itched for a pencil when a new design formed in his head. He couldn't allow himself to dwell on the desire. He wouldn't be able to get back to his career any time soon, maybe never.

"So you meant it when you moved back here. You're really going to give up your vocation, after Dad saw to it you received the education you needed." Frank bounced his fist off the wall beside him. "I suppose that means I won't be able to attend Windom Institute in Chippewa City this fall, either, even though we both know it's what Dad intended."

Jason wished Frank had chosen another time for this discussion, rather than bringing all the dirty laundry out in front of Pearl. "Not this fall, no."

Frank's jaw jutted out. "Dad was willing to chance it."

"He wasn't aware of the extent of what the newspapers are now calling the Great Economic Depression of 1893. Silver continues to fall, banks are closing all over the country. St. Paul started something they call the Public Employment Bureau—their mayor is urging farmers to hire unemployed St. Paul men," he snorted, "and that with wheat at the lowest price ever."

His brother's black eyes snapped. "Even with the price of wheat low, we're not going to starve. Dad was always one of the wealthiest farmers around. Does it make you feel powerful, keeping your tight little fist on the purse strings?"

Jason spread his palms against his thighs, trying to keep calm. "I haven't the experience Dad had running the farm. Best to set aside what money we can. Harvest isn't over; we don't know what the future might hold." He stood and reached for the newspaper on the table beside them, hoping Frank would drop the subject. "I'm going to drive into town with Pearl after supper. Would appreciate it if you'd get to work on that broken harvester."

"Why should I have to spend the evening working while you're out for an evening drive?"

Jason's hands settled on his hips. "That harvester needs to be fixed before we can get back in the fields. As for my evening drive, I'm not about to let Pearl head back alone after an afternoon of rain. You know what that can do to the roads."

Frank's square jaw tightened and Jason groaned inwardly at the battle his brother insisted on waging. "You make all the decisions around here. I can dig a buggy out of the mud as well as you, big brother. Why shouldn't you be the one to repair the machinery while I enjoy Pearl's company?"

"Fine, have it your way! *You* can spend the evening riding around in the mud and rain!"

Pearl stepped between them with a palm toward each one. "Please! I can drive myself back."

"We've had this argument before. You don't drive home alone."

A whimper broke through Jason's words and he felt a tug on his jeans. "Why are you yellin'? I don't like it when you yell."

His heart caught in his throat as he lifted Grace. "Sorry, pumpkin. Didn't mean to wake you."

"You were loud." She laid a soft little hand on his stubbly cheek, her pink lips in a pout. "I don't want you to be mad."

Jason forced a smile. The things this five-year-old did to

his heartstrings! He turned his face and kissed one of the tiny fingertips. "How could anyone be mad with you around, pumpkin?"

He hugged her close. How it cut into his soul whenever he saw her upset! He was doing a lousy job as a parent. If God was going to put him in his parents' place, it would have been nice if He'd sent him a primer on how to do the job! Setting Grace down, he gave her a tap on the back. "Go wash up for supper."

"All wight!" She hurried into the kitchen, slightly wobbly yet from her nap.

He swung his attention back to Frank. "I'll work on the harvester, and you drive Pearl back to town."

Frank turned toward Pearl, somewhat sheepishly Jason thought. "Is that acceptable to you, Pearl?"

"I always enjoy your company, Frank. In any case, it doesn't seem I have much to say about my escorts, even as to whether I shall have any."

Jason met her belligerent gaze as evenly as possible. He was tired of all the silly disagreements. *Did everyone think it was easy to run this place, to make all the decisions, to be the person responsible for all the lives the farm touched?* It made him weary all the way to his bones and he lifted a silent prayer for continued strength.

&

Pearl stood against the wall of the station house, wishing there were lamps in the area. She should probably have let her stepparents take the horse-drawn bus home, but they deserved a warmer welcome when they'd been gone for three weeks. She rather hated to meet the night train. Tramps had broken into nine box cars last week. Another night tramp had fired shots at passengers on the midnight train, then stolen potatoes and chickens waiting for shipment.

What would Jason think of her meeting the midnight train, which was infinitely more dangerous than traveling alone at night across a few miles of barren prairie. A chuckle rose in her throat at the thought.

Strange, but the railroad that the early settlers had hoped for and worked to make a reality, which brought growth to the town and prosperity to the farmers and merchants, was one of the largest causes of crime and pain in Chippewa City. Accidents among the railway workers and between trains and buggies kept her stepfather and other area doctors busy.

Were the things one hoped for always that way? Never the way one thought they would be when realized? Always accompanied by unexpected problems?

Her thoughts were interrupted by the train roaring and wheezing into town, the huge lamp on the engine lighting its way, its wheels grinding against the track as it slowed to a stop. Black coal smoke settled over the people waiting on the wide plank platform.

Lantern light framed her stepmother on the top step of the train in her gray traveling suit with a fashionable hat on her silver-striped chestnut hair. A moment later Pearl's stepfather joined her, and they descended to the platform. For an instant, Pearl lost them in the crowd. Then, pushing forward, she came face to face with them.

"Mother Boston!" She pressed her face against her stepmother's soft cheek. "Doctor Matt! It's so good to see you both again. I can't wait to hear all about the World's Fair."

The Doctor gave her a quick, tight hug, almost dislodging her smart hat with its feathers dyed to match her suit. "Reckon we'd like to hear what's happening with you first, young lady."

She laughed up at him. Goodness, she'd forgotten how tall he was! With his silvering blond hair and fair coloring, he could almost have been mistaken for the man who had given her and Johnny birth. "Nothing so exciting as Chicago and the World's Fair."

"You and Boston wait here for me. I'll get the baggage."

"Howdy, Young Doc!" An old settler greeted Dr. Matt with the affectionate term by which everyone had called him since he had first come to the area. She and Mother Boston exchanged smiles. The Doctor was a well-loved man in town. She and Johnny were fortunate he and Boston had raised them.

He returned a few minutes later loaded down with bags and they were soon on their way home. Pearl smiled broadly from the buggy's back seat. "Remember when you brought me and Johnny down to see the first train arrive in town back in seventy-eight? I thought the engine looked like a dragon from our storybooks!"

Doctor Matt didn't return her smile. "More serious dragons than that around, I'll wager."

"Matthew," Boston whispered urgently with a shake of her head, and Pearl wondered what in the world they were sending signals about.

"Did you see the Minnesota exhibits?" Pearl asked eagerly.

"Yep. The local elevator won a medal for its grain."

"That's wonderful!" It was quite an honor for the small town. She couldn't wait to tell Jason.

"Going to tell us what's been going on 'round here while we've been gone, young lady?"

"Well, the oil-tank we just passed is new. There's one on each end of town now, to make it more convenient for the night marshall to fill the lamps. And new street lamps have been placed on the hill."

"What's been happening with *you*?"

Pearl shook her head, bewildered by his unusually stern tone. "What do you mean?"

"We've been hearing tales for the last thirty miles about you and young Sterling."

"Jason?"

He nodded sharply. "Yep. Boston and I trust you, but when we hear the same tale from three different people—and respectable citizens at that. . . ."

Pearl could feel her backbone stiffening. "I haven't done anything to set people's tongues wagging."

"So you haven't been spending time at the Sterling farm?"

"Well, yes. Yes, I have."

He pulled Angel up short beneath a street lamp and both he and Boston turned to look at her. She felt blood flooding her face as she met their searching gazes.

"We're listening."

In the light of the gas lamp she could see the concern, almost fear, in his eyes beneath the determination to hear her side of the story. Boston and Doctor Matt had always played fair with her and Johnny, always trusted them to be truthful, and she knew they would listen to her now.

"So you can see it's all innocent," she finished her story. "Jason needed help, and there wasn't anyone else to give it."

"Yes, he'd tried to find a hired girl," she answered Dr. Matt's question. "And yes, Jason had refused to allow her to go out to the farm at first. But when harvest was claiming all his time and Maggie and Grace couldn't keep up with everything. . . ."

"What about Serena?" Mother Boston asked, referring to the hired Scandinavian farm girl who helped at their own home a few mornings each week.

"I asked if she could help, but she'd already hired out to another farmer for the hours she had free."

Dr. Matt urged Angel out of the light and toward the steep road that climbed the bluff to the prairie where their home was located. "Well, I can see you were just being big-hearted like Boston, here. However, a girl has to watch out for her reputation. I don't want you going out there unchaperoned anymore. Three people mentioned your visits to us tonight. *Three*!"

"But. . . ."

"Matthew is right," Boston added in her soft voice that

still had a touch of an eastern accent after eighteen years on the Minnesota prairie—and was responsible for the nickname her husband had given her. "You'll be of no use to Jason and his family if you ruin your reputation and besmirch his, also. Believe me, dear, I know how tempting it is to try to help him, but you'll have to find a more discreet manner in which to do so."

"I can't simply walk away from him now. Neither of you would pay any attention to gossip if it meant not helping a friend in need."

In the moonlight she saw Matthew's lips tighten. "You know how we've always tried to avoid making demands of you and John but I can see no other way. I refuse to allow you to return to Sterlings' farm."

Fury filled her chest at the injustice and her eyes stung from the heat of her anger. "They *need* me!"

Boston reached over the low leather seat to take her hand, and Pearl's gaze bored into hers. "Please, Mother Boston. . . ."

"Matthew is right. Proper decorum won't allow your visits. We'll have to ask the Lord to help Jason and his family some other way."

"But. . . ."

"Surely you don't think God incapable of helping them without you?"

Mother Boston's question was gentle, but her voice held a spark of laughter and Pearl had to look away. Of course God could help them without her. It was the one argument she couldn't possibly win out against.

"No." The whispered answer hurt her throat.

It wasn't that she didn't want God to help Jason. But with an unflattering, humbling glimpse into her own heart, she realized that she didn't want God to find a way to help him without her.

five

Pearl smoothed her hands over the skirt of her new, filmy butter-yellow gown as she stood beside the buggy on main street. Laughter and gay voices mingled with music from the dance in the new Rollefson building a few doors down. Excitement swirled through the evening breeze, spicy with the scent of autumn leaves. She took a shaky breath and greeted a young couple passing by.

It wasn't the music and the crowd that sent shivers tripping along her nerves, she admitted to herself. It was the knowledge that Jason would be here tonight. Only last evening she'd been at his home, yet it seemed a lifetime since she'd seen him. What would it be like if she did as Dr. Matt commanded and stayed away from the farmhouse altogether?

If she had any regard at all for her heart, she'd welcome the excuse to stay away and protect herself from heartbreak. Always before she'd thought of Jason as belonging to Miranda. Sharing Jason's struggles, knowing Miranda had rejected his marriage offer, she'd opened her dreams to what it would be like to share his life forever. Now that she'd let the hope of experiencing his love slip inside her heart, she didn't know how to push it back out.

Whatever was she going to do when Jason took a wife? Yes, she should run from all association with him. But she wouldn't, even though it meant defying Dr. Matt. With the knowledge came a clenching about her heart at the vision of pain to come.

"Haven't seen you since church last Sunday," a familiar voice said in her ear, and she turned eagerly to grasp her brother's hand.

"Johnny! Is Jewell doing well?"

A grin split his wide face beneath the hair that was as blond as her own. "She's doing fine."

"I must stop by and see her soon." A sliver of guilt poked at her. Jewell, as was proper, only left home to attend church now that she was eight months along with their first child. Usually Pearl stopped by to visit her every couple days. She hadn't been there since she had begun helping at Jason's farmstead.

Johnny was nodding. "She'd like that. I wouldn't have come tonight, but she nearly pushed me out the door. Said to be sure to come back with all the news of the neighbors, knowing everyone and their brother would be here tonight."

"Did Billy come?" she asked, referring to the orphaned eleven-year-old boy Johnny and Jewell had taken into their home when they married two years earlier.

"Not tonight." He crossed his arms and watched the passersby as he said with an exaggerated attempt to be casual, "Boston and Dr. Matt stopped this afternoon. Dr. Matt wondered why I hadn't been watching out for you better while they were in Chicago." He glanced sidewise at her.

Heat flooded her cheeks. "I haven't done anything improper."

The warmth in his gaze calmed her somewhat. "I know that. But you know how some people will imagine the worst and glory in the telling of it. Boston and Dr. Matt are only concerned for your reputation."

She nodded glumly.

He glanced over her shoulder and waved. Turning, she saw Jason coming toward them with Grace in his arms. Fireworks seemed to go off in her stomach. Dressed for the dance, his shirt blazing white against his tan, Jason looked better than ever.

Johnny and Jason visited with a comfortable familiarity while Grace talked excitedly with her. She noticed Jason studying the new two-and-a-half story brick building where the dance was being held as they talked. Was he admiring the design or thinking what he would have done differently?

"Good to see a number of brick buildings going up in town," she heard him say over Grace's chatter. "A lot safer in case of fire. Would hate to see Chippewa City lose most of its business section, like nearby Canby did recently—twenty-three business places gone overnight."

Johnny, a volunteer fireman, nodded. "Wouldn't mind seeing electrical service supplied to the town, either. It was an exploding lamp that caused the Canby fire. On the other hand, when lightning struck just fifteen miles away in Granite Falls last month and lights burst in almost every home on the electrical service, there were no major fires."

Grace demanded her attention once more and Pearl didn't hear any more of the men's conversation until the group decided to enter the dance.

Even with the cool August air and the open windows, it was hot from the swarm of people. Men's Bay Rum cologne battled with women's toilet water in fragrances of lavender, violet, and rose, and both competed with the always present cigars. Rustling gowns splashed the room with color.

Jason's laughter over a comment of Johnny's cut off sharply, his face suddenly taut. Following his shocked gaze, Pearl caught her breath. *Miranda!*

She couldn't take her eyes off her friend. Her escort, Grant Tyler, had Miranda's hand tucked intimately in the crook of his arm, and his possessive manner disgusted Pearl. Miranda's pointed chin was tilted up and she smiled boldly into his face. She'd never seen Miranda with any escort but Jason, and Grant Tyler was the last man in Chippewa City she would have suspected Miranda would agree to see.

Grant must be five years older than she and Miranda. He'd come to Chippewa City two years ago and opened a hotel—a fine one. He dressed more elegantly than most men in town, always wearing flashy vests crossed by a gold watch chain. He loved to spin that chain while watching the ladies as they passed his business establishment. Pearl always thought his smile had an oily quality to it, beneath the carefully groomed mustache that was as shiny as freshly applied shoe black. *How could Miranda refuse Jason only to turn up with this . . .this dandy?*

She darted a quick glance at Jason out of the corner of her eye. His jaw was rigid.

He set his little sister down carefully. "Will you watch Grace for a few minutes, John?" Without waiting for an answer, he took Pearl's hand. "Dance with me, Miranda."

It wasn't a question, and he didn't seem to realize he'd called her by his former fiancée's name. Pearl followed him onto the dance floor, her throat too swollen from holding back the sobs that suddenly filled her chest to protest.

The band was playing a waltz and Jason drew her stiffly into his arms. He smelled of shaving soap and his white shirt of fresh starch. She remembered ironing the shirt the day before and a queer little tightening twisted in her stomach. It had seemed such an intimate thing to do for him. Now, here she was, dancing with him, her face only inches from his broad chest covered by that same shirt and he was thinking only of Miranda.

She stumbled and Jason caught her, drawing her tight against his chest to prevent her from falling. "I'm sorry," she apologized at his look of surprise. "I've never danced a waltz before."

If he'd asked her to do him the honor of a dance, as was proper, she would have reminded him that her parents considered the waltz too intimate for unmarried couples. But he hadn't asked. He'd only assumed that of course she would dance with him, grabbed at her as a shield against the embarrassment of Miranda showing up with another man.

He grimaced. "Sorry. I forgot." The steel bands of his arms relaxed and he guided her from the floor, his hand gentle against her back.

When they reached Johnny and Grace, the little girl held up both arms to Jason. "Dance with *me!*"

Pearl thought his smile looked forced as he lifted Grace. "I'll be honored to dance with the prettiest girl here."

Grace's tiny teeth flashed with pleasure.

Jason glanced over her shoulder at Johnny. "I'm sorry," he said through tight lips. "Don't know what I was thinking, dancing with Pearl like that."

Johnny nodded solemnly.

Frank slipped up beside her as one of the townspeople claimed Johnny's attention. "Must be hard on Jason, Miranda being here with Grant and all."

"Yes." She didn't want to talk about it. It seemed disloyal to Jason. He wouldn't want people pitying him.

"Never thought anything would come between those two. Can almost forgive him for being so touchy lately."

"It's awfully warm in here. Perhaps you'd accompany me to get some punch?" Her diversion was successful. Frank took her elbow and they worked their way through the crowd to a table which had been set up to serve refreshments. After picking up their punch cups, they moved slowly about the edge of the dance floor, greeting a couple here, a group there. Scandinavian and German accents mixed with "American" accents to form a music that rivaled that of the band.

"Amy!"

Pearl heard Frank's strangled whisper at the same time she saw the willowy girl in a pink gown. Impulsively, she reached out to give her a quick hug. Next to Miranda, Amy was her dearest friend.

"I stopped by your house a few times this last week. Where have you been keeping yourself?" Amy asked in her soft voice.

The sly look that tall, skinny Ed Ray, Amy's escort, slanted at Frank did not escape Pearl and anger heated her cheeks. She looked him straight in the eyes. "I've been helping out the Sterlings. It's been difficult for Maggie, taking care of everything with their parents gone and the men in the fields."

"Oh, I do wish you'd told me! Perhaps I could have helped." Her instant, sincere response poured oil on Pearl's anger, though she noticed the distaste with which Ed greeted her words. Evidently he didn't care for the idea of Amy helping at the Sterlings.

Before she could reply, Amy reached a hand in a lacy glove to gently touch Frank's hand. It lingered on his no longer than was proper, but Pearl noticed the flush that rushed across Frank's face. "I was so sorry to hear of your loss. I've been remembering you and your family in my prayers."

"Thank you, Miss Amy," Frank murmured, his dark eyes on hers.

Ed's hand closed over Amy's elbow, drawing her away from them slightly. "Yes, Sterling, sorry to hear about your parents. Wouldn't wish it on anyone. Let's dance, Amy."

She smiled at them over her shoulder as Ed led her away.

"I understand Mr. Ray is attending Windom Institute again this fall," Pearl said, attempting to make conversation.

Frank stared broodingly after the retreating couple. "Yes. He plans to go on to the university after that to get a law degree."

She remembered his insulting look and thought she wouldn't want such a man representing the law. *Why was gentle Amy, with her high ideals, seeing him?*

"Some people have all the luck." Frank's bitter tone

surprised her. She assumed he was thinking of Jason's refusal to allow him to attend Windom Institute. Or perhaps, she thought, noticing his eyes still following Amy and Ed, perhaps he was thinking of Amy.

"What do you think of Miranda Sibley turning up on Grant Tyler's arm?"

The words seemed to scream at Pearl and Frank as they passed a group of young men, although they were spoken no louder than any of the other comments, and were not directed at them. Indeed, the speaker didn't seem aware that they were in the vicinity. Pearl and Frank exchanged glances of dismay.

"Can't blame a lady for accepting the attentions of an up-and-coming young man like Tyler. Too bad Sterling left his architectural practice to move back to the farm. What can a farmer offer her, after all?"

The others in the group nodded agreement and indignation rose in Pearl's throat. "Foolish men! Don't they know that it's farmers that keep this town and all the towns around alive?"

Frank's lips were drawn in a line so tight they might have been stitched together. "They're just repeating what they've heard. Dr. Matt says when the town was young, the farmers and townspeople were like a family, excited to build up this new land together. Now they act like enemies."

"Not all of them, but too many," he agreed. "Dad thought it was because the farmers are primarily Scandinavian immigrants, not easterners like Dad and most of the townspeople. Did you read the letter in the newspaper written by a local farmer? Says the townspeople wouldn't be crying hard times so loudly if they lived like most of the farmers—taking their children out of school and putting them to work when they need money. It's those farmers' children that lose out in the end. And just when they need to know more than ever about new farming methods and improved machinery."

His vehemence surprised her. No wonder he was so upset at not attending Windom Institute.

"Some say if a man doesn't leave the farm for an education and a profession in town, he doesn't have any future at all," he continued. "Perhaps they're right. Perhaps that's why Miss Amy is with Ed Ray. Perhaps no woman thinks there's a future with a farmer."

The hopelessness in his tone dismayed her. "Frank Sterling, no woman of value would give up a man because he's a farmer."

"Are you speaking of Miranda?"

She whirled about at Jason's question, dismay flooding her. When had he come up behind them?

"We weren't speaking specifically of Miranda." Annoyance and surprise edged Frank's statement.

Jason's eyes probed Pearl's, searching their depths in the flickering lantern light. Was he trying to decide whether she and Frank were telling the truth, she wondered, returning his gaze steadily. "It seems I owe you a second apology." His words were soft and she felt their sincerity.

Before she could respond, Jason strode away.

Pearl's hand slipped to her neck. She could feel the pulse beating there, fast as a typewriter beating out letters on one of those noisy little machines. Why did Jason have to overhear her comment? Surely he must feel that she'd insulted Miranda personally, even though she hadn't mentioned Miranda's name. First she overheard Miranda refuse him and now he overheard her effectively say that Miranda was not a woman of value. It was as though she was determined to earn his scorn.

"Hey, Sterling! What's this we hear 'bout you gettin' a new little filly out to your farm?"

Pearl's blood ran cold at the sneer in Ed Ray's voice as he

called to Jason from the group of young men. She knew instinctively he was referring to her.

Amy was nowhere to be seen. Perhaps another gentleman had claimed a dance with her, Pearl thought irrelevantly.

Beside her, Frank muttered something she couldn't understand. Pushing his empty punch cup into her hands, he started toward the men.

Jason spoke to Ed in a low voice, but though she strained, she couldn't hear his words.

"What do I mean?" the heckler asked with a laugh. "Why, that pretty little music teacher. Don't have more than one lady calling on you regular, do you?"

Dread rooted her to the spot.

six

"She's just been helping out, you say? And what kind of favors does Miss Wells do for you boys?" the awful voice rang out again. It seemed to Pearl that everyone in the vicinity had stopped to listen.

Crass laughter put wings on her feet. Dropping the punch cups heedlessly, she grasped her skirt and rushed toward the group. If they were going to insult her, they could do so to her face.

She gasped and stopped short at the sight of Frank drawing back his fist and aiming it at Ed's surprised face. Jason shoved him aside before he could land his blow and grasped Ed's narrow lapels. Every plane and line of Jason's face was rigid as he demanded in a frighteningly even voice, "I'd take back those words if I were you."

Suddenly Dr. Matt was there, looking positively spectral in the lamplight. His normally laughing eyes were like volcanoes filled with fire and fury. He grabbed tight to Jason's arm and his voice had the deceptive softness of the sheath that covers a hunter's deadly blade.

"Now, Sterling, you don't want to hit these *gentlemen*. I'm sure they were just about to apologize for their mistaken comments. Isn't that right?"

Embarrassed, the young men couldn't mutter their apologies fast enough. Jason's hold on Ed's lapels slowly released and Ed quickly followed the others in their retreat.

Would their reaction have been different if the stepfather of the woman they were deriding had not been a prominent citizen like Dr. Matt? she wondered. He had come to

Chippewa City twenty years ago, when the town was new and struggling. Like the other old settlers, he was held in awe by later citizens—the more so because of the community's love for the man who had given so much of himself to help their families over the years.

Jason's hands were balled into fists, she noticed as Dr. Matt released his arm. To think Jason had been intending to fight those—those poor excuses for men because of the statements they were making about her! Her stomach turned over at the thought. He and Frank against so many. They could have been seriously hurt because of her.

She walked toward them slowly, aware that Dr. Matt was staring at her but refusing to return his gaze. Disappointment for her loss of reputation would be in his face and she didn't want to see it. The tip of her tongue ran lightly over her suddenly dry lips. She stopped in front of the two men, but it was Jason's gaze she met, quaking. Her hands wanted to grip her skirt, to grip anything to give her added courage. She made her fingers hang quietly at her sides. "I'm sorry."

"You've no reason to apologize. You've done nothing wrong. It's those men's minds that are evil. I should have realized what I was exposing you to when I allowed you to help us out."

He turned to Dr. Matt, straightening his broad shoulders and looking him in the eye with that steady gaze of his. "I'm the one to apologize, sir, to Pearl and to you. I should have had more sense. She's a fine woman. I assure you I've made no unseemly advances toward her in the time she's been helping us and I have only the utmost respect for her. I should never have willingly exposed her to such vile speculations and comments." He swallowed hard, and Pearl saw his Adam's apple jerk. "If any man put my daughter in such a position, I expect I'd want to wallop the tar out of him."

Pearl felt her eyes widening. Why didn't Dr. Matt tell

Jason he'd never consider any such thing? She wanted to speak, but her throat seemed paralyzed.

She'd never seen Dr. Matt's face so angry. What thoughts were going on beneath his scowl?

After what seemed hours, his scowl softened slightly. "I admit the thought of a thrashing crossed my mind, but I think we can get by without it."

She heard a soft whoosh and realized Jason had been holding his breath waiting for Dr. Matt's response.

"Thank you, sir. I will never again put your daughter in such an untenable position. You have my word."

Dr. Matt held out his hand and Jason met it with his own in a solemn handshake. "I've asked her not to go to your farm again but I appreciate your taking the decision out of our hands."

Both men seemed to have forgotten she was there. Pearl took an impulsive step nearer. "Your family still needs assistance, Jason. I want to continue helping."

Disbelief washed over Jason's face. He opened his mouth to reply, then snapped it shut. A second later he spoke, his voice rigidly under control. "I appreciate your good-hearted desire to help my family, Miss Wells, but it won't be necessary."

His cold dismissal sent chills down her spine.

Matthew seemed to relent slightly at the distress in Pearl's face. He rested his large hand on her shoulder. "The fact is, Boston and I did discuss the possibility of Boston accompanying Pearl on her trips out to your place until you could arrange to hire someone to help with the housework and all."

Pearl gave a little gasp. *They hadn't told her! What a wonderful solution!*

Matthew's brows met again. "But in light of what happened here tonight, I don't think that will be possible."

"But. . .!"

"Of course not, Sir." Jason's smooth acceptance interrupted Pearl's protest. "It was kind of you and Mrs. Strong to even consider such a thing. Mighty kind."

He nodded at Pearl, and her heart ached at the stranger's face he wore. "I appreciate the help you've given more than I can say. Good night."

Dr. Matt's hand slid gently around her arm. "Come, dear. I'll walk with you to the buggy and then find Boston, so we can go home."

She stumbled once, walking as she was with her head turned over her shoulder so she could watch Jason. How could her desire to help Jason be turned into something so terrible by those young men? It seemed everything she did regarding Jason turned into a disaster lately.

Anger seethed in Jason's chest as he walked through the dance hall. How could he have been so blind? He should have realized what would happen with Pearl coming out to his home daily. It would have been different if one of his parents were alive; their presence would have protected her. But as it was—he knew men's minds, should have known what people would say. What if he'd destroyed her reputation for good? To think it took something like this to make him aware! Young men publicly ridiculing her, and her and her stepfather there to hear it.

His gaze darted about the room. He'd had more than enough "fun and relaxation" for one evening. He just wanted to find his family and start home.

Where was Frank? He'd been beside him facing that disgusting crowd outside. *When had he left?* He moved slowly about the room but after an entire trip around it, he still hadn't located him. Heading for the door, he passed Dr. Matt, still looking for his wife.

Outside again, he looked up and down the street, vainly hoping for a sight of Frank. Rows of buggies, wagons, and horses lined each side as far as he could see. People from the dance lingered in front of the building, getting some cool air.

He wandered a few feet down the plank walk, wondering where to look next, his patience growing thinner by the minute.

A scream tore through the night. *Pearl!* He raced toward the place he'd seen Dr. Matt's buggy before the dance, his shoes pounding on the wooden planks. Horses pranced and whinnied nervously, rocking buggies. A pistol shot rang out and dread scorched through him. *Please, Lord. . . .*

If only there were a lamp in this part of the street! He was vaguely aware of feet beating behind him. Another scream pierced the darkness, this time masculine.

A couple fell from the tangle of horses and buggies onto the walk, struggling wildly. Jason leaped for them, tearing the larger figure away and throwing him against the wall of a store.

"He has a gun!"

He saw the pistol glint in the attacker's hand at the same time he heard Pearl's warning. He caught the man's arm and threw it against the wall. The weapon clattered to the walk. Jason braced his body against the man, holding him captive, ignoring the oaths spewing from him on rancid breath.

In a moment other men from the dance were surrounding them. Jason gladly turned the tramp over to them, eager to see for himself whether Pearl had been harmed.

Someone lit one of the buggy's lanterns and Jason's heart spun crazily at the sight of Pearl's torn dress and dirt-smudged face. She was assuring others that she was all right, but he pushed through them and grasped her arms, needing to prove it was true.

Her eyes sparked with anger not the tears he'd been afraid he would see. She clutched the buggy whip in one hand. "Are you sure you're all right?" His voice shook.

"Yes, but. . .Jason, he was going to take the buggy, and

. . .and Angel! I couldn't let him take Angel!"

He fought a losing battle with a smile. "Of course not."

"He didn't see me in the buggy at first. When he took Angel's harness and started to lead her into the street, I took this," she held up the buggy whip, "and jumped down. He had a p. . .pistol, and I hit his arm with the handle of the whip. I. . .I didn't know how to use the other end." A small laugh escaped her. "Haven't I been telling you I can take care of myself?"

Amusement fled. Relief fueled anger. "You could have been killed! No horse is worth risking your life!"

"I couldn't let him take Angel!"

He pulled her into his arms, exasperation flooding his chest. "I can't believe you took such a foolish chance," he whispered fiercely against her neck. "Thank the Lord you're safe!"

"Sterling!"

Jason started at Dr. Matt's bellow and felt a tremor run through Pearl. He released her immediately, allowing his hands to stop at her waist only long enough to steady her.

The crowd that had formed had been concerned with the tramp and been ignoring the couple. Now they turned their attention to Jason and the Strongs, curious.

Pearl quickly explained the situation to Dr. and Mrs. Strong, needing to begin again when middle-aged, Norwegian Sheriff Amundson arrived moments later. It didn't take long for the sheriff to haul the tramp off to the jail beside the large schoolhouse on the bluff.

Dr. Matt's anger diminished when he discovered Jason had captured the tramp, but Jason knew he wasn't completely forgiven for embracing Pearl in public.

When he returned to the dance to again look for Frank, he realized that the terror he'd felt for her hadn't completely left him. It left him badly shaken. Or perhaps it was the relief of knowing she wasn't harmed.

Or the way she'd trembled in his arms and rested against him so trustingly.

Foolish thought!

Still, the memory lingered. And when Miranda moved into his line of vision, laughing at something Grant Tyler said as they waltzed past, Jason's heart didn't miss a beat.

It was two hours before Frank stumbled into the hall. His eyes were unnaturally bright and his breath smelled like a still. Jason helped him to their wagon in disgust. Just what he needed on top of everything else—a drunken brother. He'd never known Frank to drink before. Why did he have to begin now? Between that and the episode with Ed Ray, the Sterling's family name was going to be mud in town after tonight.

❧

Pearl looked about at the ripe golden wheat either side of the dusty road. Farmers were out in force today. Threshing machines hummed and whirred as numerous teams of weary draft horses circled. Chaff filled the air. Prairie chickens were everywhere, snuggling close to the wheat and wild grass or bursting into the sky in a brown rush of wings that startled Angel every time.

Almost to Jason's farm, she leaned forward slightly to glide a hand down Angel's neck. Her heart beat quicker with every passing mile. Other than church last Sunday, she hadn't seen him in the two weeks since the dance.

She'd missed him and his family horribly. Mostly him, she admitted. She'd tried to pray for him and his family whenever he came to mind, instead of dwelling on the yearning for him that seemed a constant part of her now. When the prayers were done, he lingered in her thoughts in spite of her efforts to rid them of him.

The feel of his arms about her the night of the dance, of his breath warm on her neck, would steal through her other thoughts again and again. Working with her music students didn't keep him out of her head for long. With Jewell's baby due soon, she'd spent much of her free time helping her sister-in-law with errands that were far too heavy for a woman in her condition. Even then her thoughts would stray to Jason.

After his order to stay away from the farmstead, she didn't expect him to be glad to see her. He'd be less so when he heard the reason for her visit.

Angel wanted to turn down the lane to the farmstead, knowing oats and cool water waited there. Pearl urged her on and a few acres further pulled her to a stop at the edge of a field where some men were working. Was Jason among them?

It was only a couple minutes before the men caught sight of her. One walked toward her, the wheat bending gracefully before him. It was Jason, she saw as he drew near, and her courage almost failed her. She slid off Angel's back before she could turn the horse and hurry away.

Grasshoppers jumped against her brown divided skirt, but she paid them no mind. She played anxiously with Angel's reins, wrapping the leather around her hands and unwrapping it again, watching Jason come closer.

He stopped a few feet from her and nodded a greeting. He smelled just as she'd remembered he did when he came in from the fields—of kerosene and sweat and rich earth. She wouldn't have thought the mixture could smell so sweet.

His gaze was studying her face, every inch of it, as if he'd never seen her before. It didn't help her fleeing courage to have him watching her like that.

He took a step closer and his tone was unexpectedly gentle. "Is something wrong?"

The concern in his eyes made her stomach turn over.

"It's Miranda," she blurted out. "She's engaged to marry Grant Tyler."

seven

Jason's feet seemed to have grown into the ground, as surely as the roots of the crops in his field. *Miranda actually engaged to someone else! It didn't seem possible.*

"I see."

He lifted his hat, wiped his gritty forearm across his sweaty brow and ran a hand through his hair, giving himself time to absorb Pearl's news.

"I. . .I didn't want you to hear of it from town gossip or . . .or something."

Did she think he was going to crumble under the news? He reached out absently to brush a stray lock of her blond hair behind her ear where the fragrant prairie breezes couldn't catch it for the moment.

She'd risked her father's anger and her reputation in order that he would be prepared when faced publicly with Miranda's engagement. Strange, but the engagement seemed a small thing compared to this sacrifice of Pearl's for him. He couldn't seem to stop looking at her. Dark lashes silhouetted against her creamy skin framed her wide eyes. He had to swallow twice before he could speak and then his voice sounded even to him as though it came from a cave.

"Thank you."

She nodded and leaned slightly against Angel, her hand against the horse's neck as though to steady herself.

"How is Maggie?"

Had his touch caused that breathlessness?

"Fine. Her cooking has improved considerably with your teaching."

Her smile seemed a bit feeble. "And Grace?"

Grace was another story. "She's started having nightmares. Bad ones. 'Most every night she wakes up at least once, screaming at the top of her lungs. Doesn't want any of us out of her sight during the day."

"Isn't there anything you can do?"

"Nothing we've tried has worked. Says she's afraid we'll go away and never come back, like the folks." *And like Pearl,* but he wasn't going to burden her with that knowledge. It wasn't her fault she wasn't here every day.

"I'll be praying for her. And your brothers?"

"At least they aren't having nightmares." He shrugged and tried to give a nonchalant grin.

"I've heard some rumors about Frank. . . ."

"If they're about his drinking, they're true. Don't seem to know what to do about that any more than I do Grace's nightmares."

"I'm sorry."

He was sorry, too. Seemed he was failing right and left at taking care of his family. His father would be mightily disappointed in him if he knew.

"I'd like to stop up at the house and say hello to everyone, but I'd best be getting back to town."

He nodded, wishing he had the right to ask her to stay awhile longer. But he'd promised her stepfather he'd never do anything to hurt her reputation again and he meant to keep that promise.

He watched as Pearl and Angel disappeared down the road between the wheat, barley, and corn that covered the prairie between his place and town. She'd thought he would be upset with her for telling him about Miranda and Grant Tyler; it was as plain as the turned up little nose on her round little face.

His lack of emotion at her news surprised him. There was

a time when he couldn't imagine his life without Miranda in it. It had only been a month since she'd turned him down. The longest month of his life, though not entirely because of her. He'd hardly thought of her since the dance. Only his pride had been hurt that night, not his heart. Until then, Miranda had never entered a social function on any man's arm but his or her father's.

He should have realized months ago that Miranda's feelings were changing. Whenever he'd brought up the subject of their future together, she'd become evasive. Her gaze had begun to follow other young men, particularly some of the strangers from the East who were attending the local Windom Institute.

The glimpse at Miranda's cold, selfish heart the night he proposed had destroyed the love he'd thought he had for her. It was as if she was an old habit he'd overcome. Miranda wasn't the same person she used to be, no doubt about it. She'd become someone else—someone he didn't love.

Pearl hadn't changed, except to become more of what she'd always been. More loyal, more idealistic, more beautiful. She was everything he'd wanted and expected Miranda to become.

The way she'd pitched in and helped around the house and garden—well, his family had fallen in love with her strong, cheerful spirit. Each of them complained over her absence.

He missed her, too. When he looked up a bit ago and saw her sitting atop Angel at the edge of the field, he'd thought for a moment he was daydreaming. He'd just been thinking how empty the house was without her welcoming smile when he came in from the fields.

He missed talking over little incidents of the day while he saw her home at night. He missed the comfort of knowing she was watching over his sisters and the house while he and his brothers took care of the fields and animals.

Again and again over the last two weeks pictures of her in his home filled his mind. Standing over the cookstove, darning his socks, reading to Grace, laughing at his jokes at the dinner table, her eyes meeting his in a shared smile over the tops of his brothers' and sisters' heads. She'd given him strength and encouragement and the belief that eventually life was going to be good again—just by being there, standing by all of them, and being herself. And the terror he'd felt the night of the dance when he realized she was in danger still had the power to tighten his stomach.

He rubbed the palms of his hands briskly over his face, barely noticing the bristles of his evening whiskers or the smell of the earth and wheat. Why, he loved her! Loved his best friend's little sister, the tag-along who had followed him and John around as a child, and later accompanied him and Miranda more times than he could count.

"I love her." He said the words out loud, tasting the wonder of them on his lips.

His eyes followed the road down which Pearl had disappeared. He knew she cared for him, but as a friend or older brother. Could he possibly win the love he wanted from her— the love of a woman? Or would any attempt destroy the special friendship they already shared?

&

"You're a fool, Sterling," Jason admonished himself under his breath the following evening, knocking on the screen door of Pearl's home. "The world's biggest fool, that's what you are."

He was glad it was Mrs. Strong and not Dr. Matt who answered. After the fiasco at the dance, he wasn't certain Dr. Matt would look kindly on his desire to court Pearl. He declined Mrs. Strong's invitation to step inside while she went to find Pearl, electing to stay on the porch out of Dr. Matt's way.

He ran two fingers beneath his stiff white collar. It sure was tight.

Trying to keep his freshly shined boots from clunking too loudly on the narrow wooden floorboards, he paced nervously. What if she flat out told him she wouldn't allow him to court her?

No, she wouldn't do that. They'd been friends for eight years. Good friends. She had to care for him, and a lot, or she wouldn't have been helping out at his farm, or have argued with Dr. Matt, even after Ed Ray's disgusting comments, or have come out yesterday to tell him about Miranda and Grant, or. . . .

"Good evening."

He whirled around. By Henry, she was more beautiful than he'd remembered. Her face glowed above her soft pink dress.

"Are you all right, Jason?"

With a start, he realized that he hadn't even said hello. He was acting like he'd never seen a girl before! "Hello." He swung the hat he'd been fiddling with toward the white wooden glider at one end of the porch. "Could we talk awhile?"

She preceded him to the glider, sitting down with a grace that made him all the more aware of her femininity. As if he needed a reminder! The lavender fragrance she wore contributed to the breakdown of his defenses. He slid his free hand down over his striped dress pants to wipe away the perspiration. He hadn't been this nervous since—he couldn't recall ever being this nervous.

He yanked his gaze away from hers. If he wasn't careful, he'd blurt out his love for her with no preamble. That would welcome a rejection for certain. He'd lost his parents, his career, the girl he'd once loved—his heart was too bruised to face loss again so soon.

"We've been friends a long time." The words came out in a squeaky voice that made him feel twelve years old again.

"Yes. Ever since you saved my life."

He darted a glance at her. She caught it and gave him a little smile. He forgot what he was going to say and stared at her until he felt foolish. *Had her eyes always been such a rich shade of blue?*

She looked down at her lap. "How is your family?"

"Fine." He didn't want to discuss his family. He wanted to talk about his feelings for her and find out if there was any hope of her returning his love. But he couldn't, not yet. Not without chasing her away before he even began trying to win her love. Maybe he should just say plain out that he wanted to court her. And then. . . .

"You're lucky to have each other to lean on, with your parents gone."

"Yes, I suppose we are." He snorted softly. "I'm not doing such a good job of taking care of them. Frank is always belligerent and now he's drinking every chance he gets. Maggie can't keep up with the house and garden, though she's improved after your instruction." He set his hat on the porch railing. Wouldn't be a brim left on it by the time he went home if he didn't stop rolling it up. "Fact is, the girls seem to need me more often than I can be available and half the time I don't know how to help them when I'm there."

"You're doing more for them than you realize, I'm sure." Her hand rested softly on his arm in a comforting gesture and a bolt of energy scrawled through him.

He slipped his own hand over hers, playing his fingers over her soft skin.

I love you, Pearl. The words repeated over and over in his mind and it was all he could do to keep from saying them aloud. He could tell by her tiny gasp that she was startled by his caressing touch. His declaration of love would frighten her even more. At the very least she'd think he mistook his feelings because of his grief or that he was interested in her only because he was on the rebound from Miranda.

She cleared her throat, and he lifted his gaze to her face, only inches away from his in the fading twilight.

"I wish I could help your family, Jason."

"They all miss you. They need you."

Her lashes dropped, hiding her eyes from view. He wished she'd look at him again. He couldn't seem to get enough of her eyes tonight.

The words tumbled out before he could stop them. "*I* need you. Marry me, Pearl."

eight

Marry him! Surely she hadn't heard him correctly.

But the brown eyes with the golden lights that had been dear to her for so many years were real, pleading with her. Her free hand slipped to the high lace collar of her pink organdy gown. "I. . .I don't understand."

The glider stopped, and Jason turned to face her squarely, his hands on her shoulders. "I hadn't intended to blurt it out like that. I meant to ask to court you properly. But now that it's out in the open. . . . I wouldn't ask if I thought there was a chance you were in love with someone else. You *don't* love anyone else, do you?"

"No." There'd never been anyone but Jason!

One hand cupped her cheek, and she cautiously leaned her head into it, glorying in his gentle touch. "You're certain, Jason?" Her voice trembled.

"Absolutely. We've always been good friends. We like each other, respect each other, share a commitment to keeping Christ first in our lives. We'd be good together."

"Yes." Did he honestly think she needed to be argued into marrying him? A smile hovered on her lips.

His grin filled his face, and something she'd never seen before sparked in his eyes, taking her breath. His hands cradled her face, making it impossible to look away from him. "Does that mean you'll marry me?"

She wondered if her smile was as wide as his. "Yes."

He took a deep breath and its shakiness made her feel humble. Did he care for her so much? She ached to speak her love for him, but daren't unless he spoke first. "I wasn't expecting. . .I mean. . .you've always loved Miranda. We've only been friends."

Silence hung between them until she didn't think she could bear it any longer. One of his hands slipped to cover hers where they clasped in her lap. His skin was callused and cut from working with the wheat, but even so she welcomed his touch.

He began to say something, then stopped and cleared his throat. Why, he was as nervous as she was! The thought brought a smile. She'd never seen him nervous before. Always he seemed so sure of himself. It was one of the things she admired in him. But to think he was nervous at proposing to her made her feel tender toward him and she caressed the back of his hand with her thumb.

"You're right, we've only been friends. I want you to be my wife, but I'll not force my. . .attentions on you."

Something deep within her froze. He wasn't asking her to marry him because he loved her.

How was it possible to hurt so deeply when she felt completely empty inside? She made herself look him full in the face, hoping he wouldn't see her disappointment, willing her voice to be steady. "I understand. A friendly marriage. To look after your home and family."

Something flickered in his eyes and was gone. Was it regret? Surely not. She was being fanciful.

"Yes. A friendly marriage."

"Are. . .are you trying to use me to hurt Miranda?"

He touched her cheek again, caressing it lightly with his knuckles. "No. I need you."

His words were barely a whisper and the urgency in them made her want to reach out to comfort him, but she couldn't move.

"Do you want to change your mind?"

He'd said he needed her. To turn him down would be unthinkable! "No."

"Sunday."

"What?"

"Let's get married Sunday."

"But that's only two days away!"

"Do you want a big wedding?"

Of course she did. Every girl she knew wanted a big wedding. But if he wanted to be married Sunday, that settled it. "Sunday will be fine. That is, is it possible to purchase the license and arrange for Uncle Adam to marry us by then?" She was amazed she could even consider such practical things.

"The license will be no problem, and I can't imagine Rev. Conrad not finding time to marry his favorite niece."

They talked for an hour, discussing their arrangements and when her things would be moved to the farmstead—her clothing, her hope chest, the few pieces of china that had belonged to her mother.

When he walked her to the door he drew her close to him and her hands trembled slightly on his shoulders. His lips touched her temple so lightly and quickly that she wondered if she'd imagined it. "I'll be a good husband to you, I promise."

A good husband, she thought as she watched him walk swiftly to his horse, *but not a husband who loves his wife.* The knowledge squeezed her heart unbearably.

The starry night surrounded Jason as he rode home. His saddle creaked and the insects made prairie music, a background to the song in his heart. She'd promised to marry him. Forty-eight hours from now she'd be his wife.

A friendly marriage. He'd only wanted to reassure her that he wouldn't push her too quickly from the role of friend to that of wife. But one day, he'd win her love—the love of a woman for a man.

Anything less was unthinkable.

❧

What could Miranda possibly want, Pearl wondered Saturday evening. She sat on the edge of the cushion at one end of the green velvet sofa in her parents' parlor and looked at

Miranda sitting on the other end. They hadn't spoken to each other since the evening Miranda turned down Jason and slapped Pearl's face. She could feel the sting of it even now.

Miranda was dressed in a fashionable visiting suit of russet silk with tan shoes and matching bag. One of the wide hats she loved perched on her gleaming brown hair. She was beautiful, in a dark, vivid way with which her own pale beauty could never compete, Pearl realized with a twinge.

Her friend's eyes darted about the room curiously and Pearl knew she was taking in the preparations for the wedding to be held in the parlor the next afternoon. She waited patiently for Miranda to state the purpose of her visit. Manners dictated that she offer Miranda some refreshment but there were limits to her hospitality. She didn't want to encourage Miranda to stay any longer than necessary.

Miranda's brown eyes met hers and she lifted her chin a trifle. "Even though we haven't been very friendly lately, I wanted to tell you my news myself. I'm engaged to be married. To Mr. Grant Tyler."

Her eyes held the look of a Roman conqueror, Pearl thought with distaste. "Yes, so I've heard."

Miranda's lips formed a little pout. "Oh, dear, and I did so want you to hear the news from me." With a practiced feminine shrug that lifted the lace on the shoulders of her gown, she dropped her lashes in false modesty that tightened the corners of Pearl's mouth. "I suppose it's difficult for people not to speak of the wedding plans of one of the town's most eligible bachelors."

There was a time Miranda would have thought such behavior as unbecoming as she thought it herself, and Pearl couldn't help but wish her old sweet friend were with her now instead of this preening creature.

"I've heard rumors that you're engaged, also. To Jason. Of course, I told the rumor-bearer that was impossible." In spite of her attempt to appear unconcerned, her eyes peered sharply at Pearl.

"We're to be married tomorrow."

They stared at each other for a full minute. Sounds of the neighborhood filtered through the screens to enter on the breeze that lifted the lace-edged curtains: children laughing, horses' hooves plodding through the streets, buggy wheels creaking, dogs barking. But from the parlor, there was no sound at all.

"You can't be serious."

"Why?"

"Jason loves me! He's always loved me."

"You told him you wouldn't marry him. I heard you myself."

Miranda had also said that she still loved Jason, and would agree to marry him when he "came to his senses." Had Jason returned to her after that night, repeating his proposal? Would she ever know?

The buttons and lace on the front of Miranda's gown rose and fell rapidly. "What kind of friend are you, that you would marry him?"

"The kind of friend who will not turn him down because he plans to stay on his parents' farm and care for his family."

"Have you no pride? Jason would marry me even now if I'd have him."

She was right, of course. The knowledge of it hadn't left Pearl for a moment since Jason admitted theirs was only to be a friendly marriage. She'd never give Miranda the satisfaction of knowing she believed it. "If you prefer Jason to Mr. Tyler, then I encourage you to tell Jason so. It's not kind to either man to marry Mr. Tyler if you love Jason."

Miranda rose swiftly. "And live on a farm with a ready-made family? I should say not!"

Pearl stood slowly, her eyes never leaving Miranda's flashing brown ones. "No," she said quietly, relief mingling with her pain. "I didn't think you would."

nine

Boston patiently completed joining the myriad of tiny buttons that ran up the back of Pearl's white chiffon bodice while Pearl stared at her reflection in the freestanding floor-length mirror in her bedroom. Her fingers played with the orange blossoms that trailed down each side from the large bow at her neck to the hem of her skirt. The blossoms' scent surrounded her.

"The gown is lovely, Mother Boston."

Mrs. Strong turned her around and fussed with the pale yellow that edged the waist of the white brocade satin skirt. She stepped back, a satisfied smile slipping across her face beneath the coronet of still thick chestnut brown hair streaked with gray. "Yes, I dare say it is."

Pearl gave her an impulsive hug. "Do you feel cheated out of planning a large wedding?"

"Not for myself. But a wedding planned on two days' notice. . ." Boston wrinkled her nose. "It's not what I have always wanted for you."

"You didn't have a grand wedding and your marriage has weathered the years beautifully."

"Yes, life with Matthew has been very good." The tender, faraway look in her stepmother's eyes made Pearl's chest ache.

"Jason is a fine boy," Mrs. Strong continued, fitting a plain, filmy, floor-length veil on Pearl's head. She began anchoring a row of orange blossoms across the top with hairpins. "But your decision to marry was made in such haste."

Pearl kept her gaze determinedly on the high lace collar of the mauve gown that lent a lovely shade of rose to Boston's face.

70

"There!" Her stepmother stepped back. "What a beautiful bride!" She took Pearl's hands in her own. "I don't wish to pry, dear, but I do so desire your happiness. Do you love Jason?"

Pearl returned her gaze steadily. She didn't have to avoid the truth to give the answer she knew her stepmother wanted to hear. "Very much."

"Does he return your love?" Her voice held an apology.

Pearl picked up the bouquet that was lying on her bed. "He's never said so."

She heard Mrs. Strong's shaky breath. "Then why are you marrying him?"

"He needs me, he and his family."

Pearl could feel the love emanating from the woman who had raised her. "My dear, have you any idea how difficult life will be married to a man who doesn't love you?"

She picked at the blossoms of her bouquet restlessly. "You've always taught me to trust God's Word. Remember I Corinthians 13:7? Charity 'Beareth all things, believeth all things, hopeth all things, endureth all things.'"

"The verse does not imply that these attributes of love come either easily or painlessly." Her lifeworn hands bracketed Pearl's face and her voice gentled. "Marriage is sacred and meant to last a lifetime. That's a long time to be unhappy."

"I refuse to be unhappy with Jason. We've always been fond of each other. Perhaps one day that fondness will grow to love."

"Loving someone doesn't ensure that love will be returned. If it could, everyone on earth would return God's love."

Why won't she stop? Pearl wondered desperately. "Sometimes, loving someone *can* bring love in return. Doesn't the Bible tell us in I John 4:19 that 'We love him, because he first loved us'?"

The tears in her stepmother's eyes hurt her. She slipped

her cheek next to the older one. "I want to be strong and cheerful for Jason always. With God's help, I can be. It's my wedding day. Be happy for me, please."

Boston gave her a quick squeeze before pulling back to look into her face. "When you and Johnny became part of our lives, I was afraid you would never heal from the pain of losing your parents so young. It became Matthew's and my prayer that one day you would not only be healed, but that God would use you to heal other lives. Now Johnny helps heal lives by managing the poor farm and you are to be part of God's healing for Jason and his family."

Pearl felt Boston's hands tremble as she ran her fingertips along the veil where it framed her cheeks. "It appears God has answered our prayers. But I wonder if I would have been brave enough to ask it, if I'd known the cost it would demand of you."

Pearl's blue eyes met Boston's brown ones. "Would you have me be otherwise?"

Boston shook her head slowly. "No. Matthew and I couldn't be prouder of the lovely, Christlike woman you've become." A tender smile filled her eyes and her hands rested on Pearl's shoulders. "If you can believe God will fill Jason's heart with love for you, then I will join you in your prayer, and believe with you."

The ceremony had been mercifully quick, Pearl thought, looking about at the small group of people chattering cheerfully in the flower-filled parlor. Except for her bridesmaid, Amy, only her own family, Jason's family, and Rev. Conrad's family had been invited. She was glad. It was difficult enough acting as though this was a normal wedding. The strain of it was getting on her nerves.

"You're the most beautiful bride I've ever seen!"

Pearl smiled at Maggie's wide eyes and eager compliment, remembering well that all brides look beautiful to a twelve-year-old girl.

"I'll second that."

Heat flooded her face at Jason's words. He laughed and raised his eyebrows. "A blushing bride. Now that's a pleasant sight."

She turned away amid Maggie's giggles. If she weren't the object of his jest, she'd be glad to see him teasing and laughing again, like the man she knew before his parents died. His arm slipped possessively about her waist and her heart raced.

He'd been acting the part of the happy bridegroom since she'd joined him in front of Uncle Adam to exchange their vows. Why? Did he want people to think they were like any normal couple, wildly in love? If that was what he wanted, she would go along with it.

Johnny and Jewell were suddenly beside her and Johnny leaned down to give her a peck on the cheek. "My little sister married. Thought I'd never see the day."

"Well, I like that!" Pearl said indignantly, her hands propped at the waist of her satin skirt.

"Johnny!" Jewell reproved softly at the same time.

Johnny ignored their outbursts. "Remember a couple years ago when I tried to give you some advice on men, little sister?" He grinned broadly at Jason. "She told me in no uncertain terms that she could judge men just fine herself. Have to admit she's done a better job of it than I thought she would." He held out his hand to Jason. "Welcome to the family, old man. No one I'd rather see Pearl marry."

"Couldn't agree with that sentiment more." Jason pulled her even closer to his side. She forced herself to relax against him as though she was accustomed to being there. "I only hope we'll be as happy together as you two."

She wished that, too! *If only he meant it.* Of course he wanted them to be happy together, but not truly as man and wife.

"Are you ready to leave, Mrs. Sterling?"

Her new title on Jason's lips sent shivers dancing along her arms. He was smiling into her eyes, with a warmth tinged with laughter. Anyone who didn't know better would think he actually cherished her as a new husband would be expected to do.

At Pearl's suggestion, Maggie took Grace upstairs during the leave-taking. She and Jason feared the girl would be upset if she saw them driving away. Maggie had been told that Grace could have her choice of Pearl's dolls. They hoped the gift would keep the girl calm for the evening.

He guided her toward the door, family members from both sides stopping them every couple steps for a reminder or a hug or words of well wishes.

Rev. Conrad rested a hand on Jason's shoulder and held one of Pearl's hands. She looked up into his kind, deep-set eyes. His voice rumbled in its usual deep manner through the dark beard tinged with gray. "Proverbs 18:22 says that 'Whoso findeth a wife findeth a good thing, and obtaineth favour of the Lord.'" He gave them one of his rare smiles.

Mrs. Conrad, slightly plump but stylish, slipped a dainty hand through his arm. "Does the Bible say it's a good thing for a woman to find a husband?"

His large hand cupped hers and the tender look he gave her caught at Pearl's heart. "Not that I've found, I'm afraid."

"I thought not. However," Mrs. Conrad glanced up at her husband from the corner of her eye, "I've found a husband to be a good thing, just the same."

Matthew leaned down to hug Pearl. "I hope you find it so, too," he said in a low voice. He straightened and reached to shake hands with Jason. "See you're good to her."

"I'll do my best to make her happy, sir."

It sounded like a solemn vow, the way he said it, Pearl thought. Her emotions had been swinging like a chandelier in the wind all day but for the first time tears filled her eyes.

"See that you do," Matthew said gruffly.

Pearl hugged Boston good-bye and then Jason was helping her into the decorated carriage, and they were moving swiftly down the street behind Angel, the younger family members running along, calling cheers and good-byes.

They were at the edge of town before the well-wishers dropped back. The further they moved out into the prairie, the more strained the silence became between the two. Pearl wished fervently that Jason hadn't arranged for his brothers and sisters to spend the evening at her home—that is, at her stepparents' home. More of his charade that their marriage was normal.

They hardly exchanged two words on the drive and Pearl was glad when they finally arrived at the farmstead. Twilight had faded and she remained in the carriage while Jason went inside to light some lamps.

When he returned, he helped her down, then reached for her alligator-skin valise. Frank would bring the rest of her things when he and the others returned the next day. The valise looked so small, carried so few of her belongings, that she felt vulnerable.

"You'll have Mom and Dad's room," Jason said, leading the way upstairs. "Maggie readied it for you."

He held the door to the room and she entered timidly. She'd never been in this room. Always when she'd been in the house, the door had been closed. Maggie had told her none of the family wanted to disturb it, feeling it would be too painful, too final.

"Are you sure you want me to stay in here?"

Jason set the valise on the end of the bed, not looking at her. "Yes."

The room was larger than the other bedchambers and had a matching set of fine cherry furniture. The bed was veiled in

Nottingham lace and a lace scarf lay across the dressing table. A china pitcher trimmed in gold with delicately painted violets sat in a matching bowl on the stand beside the lace-covered windows. Mauve-colored, patterned paper warmed the walls.

"It's a lovely room." She recalled Jason telling her how his father had loved to give his mother beautiful things. He'd certainly filled their personal room with beauty.

Jason had lit the lamp on the dressing table and the flame shone through the etched glass of the globe to reflect off the mirror, multiplying the light. A porcelain vase stood beside the lamp, filled with wild flowers whose fragrance scented the room. She touched one of the blossoms, aware of Jason standing in the doorway watching her. "Did Maggie pick these, too?"

"I did."

Something he'd done unbidden, just for her. Not to fool their families, but to welcome her. She wanted to gather the vaseful and hug the flowers close to her chest, burying her face in them. "Thank you."

He nodded and crossed the room to open the doors of the large clothes press. She was surprised to see it empty. "Maggie packed up Mom and Dad's things so you can put your clothes wherever you please. The room is entirely yours."

"It must have been difficult for Maggie, putting away your parents' things. I'd have helped her if I'd known."

Jason was beside her in two steps, sweeping her into his arms. "I think the Reverend was right." His husky voice set her nerves tingling. "A wife is a good thing." She felt his lips press against her neck and then he released her, moving to the door so quickly that she almost lost her balance.

He stood silhouetted there a moment, staring at her. "I'm sorry, it won't happen again. I'd best put Angel up."

But he didn't leave and Pearl wished she could see his face

clearly in the lamplit room. What had he meant by taking her in his arms that way, chasing her breath away?

"I'll be sleeping in the same room as always, with Frank and Andrew across the hall. If you need anything, just call."

He pulled the door shut behind him. She stood where she was, listening to his footsteps go down the stairs and fade. The outside door slammed a moment later.

Shakily she sat down on the edge of the bed, trying to catch her breath. Though his arms had been around her so briefly, she could still feel their warmth and strength. Was he sorry he'd embraced her so intimately in her bedchamber?

She reached for her valise and removed the white muslin bridal set her stepmother had purchased for her the day before. Her fingers drifted lightly over the tucks and fine embroidery and Hamburg lace. She hadn't had the courage to tell Mother Boston there wouldn't be any need for new nightwear.

Part of her was relieved that Jason was sleeping elsewhere but she hadn't expected to feel so incredibly lonely. It was silly, considering she'd been sleeping alone most of her life.

Was Mother Boston right? Had she been a fool, marrying a man who didn't return her love?

She wrapped her arms about herself tightly, trying to relieve the pain inside her. "Please, Lord, help me. Help me to keep loving Jason, and hoping and believing and enduring, as Your word says. Help me to be a good wife to him. And please, please take away some of this pain."

She brushed a tear from her cheek impatiently and began to change. It took her a full half-hour to undo the six dozen tiny buttons at the back of her bridal gown. A number of times she considered asking Jason to assist her, but the memory of his lips against her neck warned her that it wouldn't be wise.

In her fine new chemise and drawers, she folded back the

covers of Jason's parents' bed, then turned to put out the lamp. Something on the wall above the bed caught the corner of her eye and she looked back.

It was a sampler. She leaned across the bed, trying to read it, but the lamplight didn't reach that far. Picking up the lamp, she lifted it in front of the embroidered piece.

"Charity hopeth all things," she read. A chill shivered through her, and the roots of her hair felt as though they were charged with lightning. A phrase from the verse she'd quoted to Mother Boston earlier that day!

She returned the lamp to the dressing table. Before putting it out, she pulled a stem from the vase of wildflowers. A sweet peace filled her as she slipped between the clean, crisp sheets and drew the soft, fragrant blossom lightly across her cheek.

The tightness that had made her insides feel like coiled wire all day long began to release. Surely God was showing her through Jason's mother's sampler that He would answer her prayer for Jason's love. She was to continue believing and hoping. God would make this strange, funny marriage right. She just had to continue hoping. . . .

ten

Jason tugged at Angel's lead, pulling her into a stall, oblivious to the crunching of straw beneath his best shoes, his work team's welcoming whinnies, or the sound of mice scurrying in the corners.

He'd had it all planned out—to go slowly, keep things casual and cheerful between himself and Pearl as they had always been, to allow her to become comfortable in his home and with his constant presence. Then, slowly let her know of his love, as though they were courting.

Instead he'd pulled her into his arms with no warning at all. Her eyes were huge when he looked back at her from the relative safety of the bedchamber door. Had he frightened her? Did she think he was going back on his word?

Well, he wouldn't. God help him, he'd stick to his original plan. He'd never take her to his bed unless she loved him as a wife loves a husband.

Leaning against the fence beside the barn, he stared moodily at the house. *My wife is there.* Wonder filled him at the thought. She'd been so beautiful in her wedding dress. Her eyes and voice hadn't wavered as she'd taken her vows. It was up to him to see she didn't regret those vows. Life wasn't going to be easy for them, but that didn't mean it couldn't be good.

Lord, please let her return my love. It was clear from the scriptures that it was the Lord's will that husbands and wives love one another. Surely God would answer his prayer. Until then, Pearl would be in his home, sharing his life. He wanted more, he thought restlessly, but it was enough for now.

a

Pearl slipped a final tomato into the bushel basket setting beside her between the garden furrows and stood, her hands against the small of her back as she unkinked her muscles. A red-winged black bird lit on a plant, cocked his head at her and darted off, his wing a crimson and black splash against the sky. A frown knit her brow beneath the wide straw hat she wore to protect her skin. Clouds rolled over and under each other like milk in a churn, constantly shifting shades of gray. It was going to rain, and hard. The only question was how soon. The stillness preceding the storm was eerie; winds were one of the constants on the prairie.

"Come along, Grace." Lifting the basket, she started for the house with Grace racing stumbingly through the garden row before her.

Funny how her attitude toward the weather changed after only a few days on the farm. In town a storm was merely an inconvenience, causing errands and pleasure outings to be postponed and making the streets difficult to pass. Here, a storm could threaten her new family's livelihood.

A smile softened the tense muscles in her face. Her new family. Precious words.

On the porch, she turned and surveyed the fields. She knew the men would stay out until the storm struck, redeeming every available minute.

She set the basket down inside the pantry. Spices in round wooden boxes, coffee in its red tin, and the ever-present kerosene jug dwarfed the smell of the fresh vegetables. She'd have to find time to preserve what vegetables she could for the winter. Perhaps Boston would help her; it would give them a chance to visit.

Pearl moved to the screen door. The clouds seemed to meet the earth in a solid gray-blue wall not far past Thor Lindstrom's fields.

Jason had told her to expect some neighbors to join himself and the day laborers next week to help with the threshing. Thor's wife, Ellie, had stopped the day after the wedding, offering to assist Pearl in cooking for the large group of men. She was grateful for the offer and would return it when the threshers worked Thor's farm.

Jason's favorite team of draft horses, fly nets flapping, stomped rapidly into the yard pulling a load of grain and the three men. The wind was already increasing, and whirled the wheat from the wagon in dusty sworls. Even as she watched Jason and Andrew leap down to open the barn doors so Frank could drive the wagon inside, darkness shut out the daylight.

Rain came pouring down, the wind whistling around the house with a ferocious intensity.

Boots rushed across the porch and the kitchen door swung open before the men. They were soaked to the skin and water poured from their hats and clothes. Pearl was surprised to find that the day laborers had already left, hoping to beat the storm home.

When the men had changed, Maggie poured fragrant coffee from the large granite-ware pot and set out sugar cookies, and the family spent a few luxurious minutes visiting around the kitchen table. Grace sat on Frank's lap and happily dunked a cookie in his coffee cup until the cookie all but dissolved. The little girl always loved when the men returned from the fields.

So did she, Pearl admitted to herself.

Frank pulled out the latest edition of *The Progressive Farmer* and Andy slipped away—likely to bury his nose in another dime novel, Pearl thought. Grace climbed on Maggie's lap in the rocking chair and listened entranced to *Black Beauty*.

Jason took his cup of coffee and went out on the porch, leaned against a pillar, and watched the rain still drenching the land. Pearl took her blue cotton shawl from the pegs behind the kitchen door and followed him, pulling the door shut behind them. She tugged the shawl close about her shoulders as she went to stand beside him, tucking a hand in his arm in the comfortable old familiar manner she'd had with him when they were young, and fiancés and marriages were far in their future.

"Will the rain damage the crops?"

Jason slipped his arm from her hand to drop it loosely about her shoulders. "Dad always said not to tally up your losses until the game was over, but it doesn't look good."

It felt warm and secure with his arm about her, and she leaned against him contentedly.

He sighed deeply. "A farmer's always at nature's mercy. How's a man supposed to care for a family, never knowing when some storm or insects might wipe out his crops?" His hand cupped her shoulder, drawing her closer against him. "And now I've dragged you into that life."

She slipped a hand cautiously over his, not wanting to let him know how intimate it felt to be so near him. "I wasn't dragged into this m. . .marriage kicking and screaming. I'm not meant to be a responsibility. Wives were created to be helpmates, if I remember the story of Adam and Eve correctly."

His chuckle rumbled in her ear. "That's a mean argument. Makes it difficult for me to stand up on my soap box and orate on man's natural superiority."

"Good!"

"But I've made a commitment to my brothers and sisters, and they're counting on me."

"God has made a commitment to you, too."

He was silent a moment. "I needed that reminder to trust Him. I've felt like Atlas trying to carry the earth on his shoulders the last few weeks. And doing a poor job of it, too."

The door creaked open behind them. Pearl tried to ignore the disappointment that flickered through her at the interruption.

"Pearl, will you cut my hair tonight?" Maggie asked, frowning down at one of her braids. "You did promise, and school is starting soon."

Jason jerked around, and a lonely feeling settled in the pit of Pearl's stomach as his arm dropped from her shoulders. "Why are you cutting your hair?"

"I'm almost thirteen. Girls my age simply do not wear their hair in braids."

"If you wear your hair short, how are the guys at school going to stick your braids in the inkwells or pull on it to let you know they've got a hankering for you?"

Maggie's face flooded with color. "Boys! Really, Jason!"

Pearl fought back a smile. "I recall a certain young man dunking my braids in an ink well. Ruined my favorite school dress." Her gaze darted accusingly to Jason, and she had the satisfaction of seeing him flush. "If you find some shears, I'll cut your hair now, Maggie."

She was back in a minute with a comb and shears, and they all moved to the kitchen.

Jason sat across the table from them, turning the pages of the Montgomery Ward Implement Catalog. "So what's this newfangled hairstyle like?"

"Didn't you notice that almost all the young misses at the dance were wearing their hair in loose curls just below their shoulders?"

"Can't say I did, Sis."

"Men!"

"You have to remember, I'm a married man. I'm not supposed to be noticing other girls."

Pearl's hands stilled and her gaze shot to Jason's. He'd been waiting for it, his eyes laughing at her. The comb trembled slightly as she began pulling it through Maggie's hair once more. "We weren't married then."

He chuckled and she had to smile. She'd sounded like a prim, middle-aged housewife even to herself.

Maggie pulled a Jordan Marsh catalog from the stack of magazines Jason had brought into the room and showed him the current style.

Grace entered and dumped two dolls and an armload of homemade clothes on the wooden chair beside Jason. Picking up a curly-haired doll, she wrapped it with painstaking care in a soft flannel square, then leaned heavily against Jason's leg. "She needs you to hold her."

Jason took the doll in his arms as carefully as though it were a baby and Pearl's heart turned over at his gentle care for his little sister's feelings. She well remembered how Johnny refused to have anything to do with her when she played with dolls. "Pretty baby. Don't remember seeing her before. Is she new?"

Grace nodded, her head bouncing repeatedly, her attention already on another doll she was awkwardly attempting to diaper with a flannel scrap. "Pearl gave her to me."

"What's her name?"

"Mawy."

"Mary? Nice name."

Would Grace never outgrow her difficulty with the 'r' sound, Pearl wondered as the little girl answered Jason. "Yes. That's her name 'cause Pearl gave her to me on your mawwy day."

A frown puzzled on Jason's brow. "You mean the day Pearl and I got married?"

The bouncing nod repeated. "Maggie said Pearl won't ever leave us again. She said when people get mawwied, they stay together for always." Her eyes looked like big brown buttons as she raised them seriously to Jason's face, silently asking if it was true.

He pulled her into his lap. "That's right, pumpkin. When people get married, they make promises to each other. You know what promises are, don't you?"

"Yes. That's when you can never change your mind."

Pearl saw a laugh twinkling in the eyes so like Grace's. "That's a pretty good way to look at a promise, I reckon."

"And you pwomised to stay with Pearl for always?"

"Yep."

"What else did you pwomise?"

His voice grew softer and there was a hint of huskiness. "I promised to love Pearl, and honor her, and cherish her forever."

Grace tilted her head and poked a finger at his chest, accentuating each word. "And you can't ever change your mind."

Pearl's heart caught in her throat as he captured her gaze in his. "No, I won't ever change my mind."

"Good." Grace wriggled down from his lap and exchanged dolls with him. "Now you hold Molly for awhile."

"Yes, ma'am," he said meekly.

Pearl could hardly keep her mind on trimming Maggie's hair. Why was he doing this, repeating his vows as though he meant them with all his heart, when they both knew it was Miranda he loved?

Pain lanced through her. How sweet it would be if his vow to love her had been sincere! It must have been difficult for him to promise to love and cherish her, when his heart belonged to another. He wasn't a man to give his word lightly.

Grace seemed content to play silently beside Jason and he turned back to teasing Maggie. "Almost thirteen sounds a little young to be interested in boys."

"I didn't say I was interested in boys!"

"My mistake."

Big brothers must all be cut from the same cloth, Pearl thought, remembering how Johnny had teased her through the years. About time she came to Maggie's rescue. "You weren't much older than Maggie when you met. . . ."

"My wife." He smoothly cut off her reference to Miranda. She stared at him over Maggie's head, her mouth open slightly. What had come over him today? Perhaps he was simply his normal teasing self and had no idea how her heart turned each word over and over, wishing for his love.

"Tell me how you met," Maggie demanded.

"It was the winter your family moved here." Pearl clipped at the long locks carefully. "We were skating on the river. I skated too far downstream and fell through some weak ice. Jason rescued me."

Maggie gasped and whirled around, her eyes huge and shining. "He saved your life? How *romantic*!"

"Your hair is going to be much shorter than you wish if you jerk like that again." She softened the words with a smile. "It wasn't romantic at all. I looked like a drowned rat."

"You didn't look quite *that* bad," Jason qualified gallantly.

"Anyway, it took me a minute to find the hole in the ice when I came back to the surface of the river. I tried to crawl out, but the ice was too thin, and kept breaking off. My hands felt like icicles, and my body was growing numb quickly. Then I heard Jason telling me to keep fighting."

She stopped trimming, the memory so powerful she couldn't continue.

Jason shrugged. "It wasn't such a big thing."

"I could hear the other kids yelling at him to stay back or he'd fall in, too, but he didn't even take his eyes off me once. He just flattened himself against the ice and held out a stick and told me to grab on. My hands were too cold by then to close around something that small."

"What happened next?" Maggie asked breathlessly.

She looked at the eyes that had stared into hers that long-ago day, knowing her heart was in her gaze but not knowing how to prevent his seeing it. "He said not to worry, he wasn't going to let me die." *And then the sun came out.* She always remembered it that way. His eyes had been brown and warm and golden all at once, like the sun. She'd looked into them and known he wouldn't let her drown and the panic inside her ebbed away.

"You're making me sound way too gallant. You should be writing serials."

Pearl ignored his modesty. "He crawled closer to the edge of the hole. We could hear the ice cracking with every movement. My brother, John, who had been too far away to get to us immediately, held onto Jason's skates in case Jason fell in, too. It was a good thing, as the ice broke two more feet around the hole before Jason pulled me out."

Maggie sighed and hugged her arms around her apron-covered chest. "It's just like the knights of the round table."

Jason choked on his coffee, and Pearl laughed at him over Maggie's head. "Knights! Do I look as if I wear armor?"

"You're a hero just the same," Maggie said with a determined nod of her freckled round face. "Overalls and all."

Jason snorted and refused to meet either of their gazes.

"He's certainly a hero in my book. I tagged after him for months." *Years would be more accurate,* Pearl thought. She handed Maggie a hand mirror. "What do you think of your new look?"

Maggie lifted a hand to the wavy hair. "Is it really me?"

Jason picked up the catalog Maggie had shown him earlier. Pursing his lips, he looked critically from the page to Maggie and back again. "Yep. You look just like the young miss in the advertisement."

Maggie flushed with pleasure.

"We'll wrap your hair on rags this evening to make curls."

"Oh, Pearl, I'm so glad you came to live with us!" She wrinkled her nose at Jason. "And I don't care what you say. I think it's the most romantic thing I've ever heard, meeting your wife by saving her life."

"Just hope your own life doesn't ever need saving," Jason grumbled as he stood up. "Far from being the fearless savior Pearl describes, I was scared out of my wits the whole time."

"I never knew that."

Pearl didn't realize she'd said the words aloud until he stopped beside her. "Any reasonable person would have been. I was shaking in my boots; scared stiff you were going to sink beneath the waterline and be gone forever." His trembling attempt at a smile made her throat ache. "And then who would have been my helpmate?"

Her knees lost their starch as he left the room, and she plopped into the chair beside Maggie. Jason had always been an irrepressible tease. If she didn't stop taking his comments seriously, she was going to make herself miserable.

But his words and intense gaze lingered in her mind the rest of the evening and followed her into her bed that night. "I promised to love Pearl. . .forever."

eleven

The night of the big storm was the last Pearl had time to dwell on Jason's behavior. The storm hadn't been as damaging as they'd feared. Crop losses were minimal, though they later learned that many farmers did lose crops and windows to hail—including the poor farm Johnny managed.

It was days before the land dried out enough for the men, horses, wagons, and machines to get back into the fields. Until then they spent their time repairing and maintaining fences and machinery, and cleaning out the barn. Once they were back in the fields, Pearl and the girls seldom saw the men other than at meals, or when they carried morning and after-noon snacks to them.

Preserving, cooking, baking, laundry, housekeeping, and gardening kept the women as busy as the men. The hired men merely added to Pearl's work load. She fell into bed each night so tired that she was asleep almost before she fin-ished her prayers.

Sundays were the only times of rest. After church they would often visit with Dr. Matt and Boston, or with Johnny and Jewell. Back at the farm, the children loved to read. Sometimes they had hay fights in the barn, or slid down the haystacks—which would set Grace to giggling non-stop. Pearl especially liked the times they went horseback riding. She missed riding Angel and the horse was gaining weight from lack of exercise.

Rising before the sun was especially difficult for Pearl, but always Jason arose before her and had the fire in the kitchen stove started so she could prepare the usual huge breakfast.

His thoughtfulness never failed to add cheer to her morning.

Pearl's hope dipped and swayed like the wheat in the wind the first few days of their marriage, and she asked the Lord to show her how to stay strong in the hope He'd given her on her wedding night. Soon after, she came across Romans 15:4 in her daily devotions: "For whatsoever things were written aforetime were written for our learning, that we through patience and comfort of the scriptures might have hope."

The verse excited her and she determined that she would not miss her daily devotional time regardless of her busy days. Sometimes she could fit in no more than ten minutes. She decided to make hope the topic of her devotions. Reading of God's faithfulness in keeping His promises to His people throughout the centuries encouraged her to keep hoping for Jason's love.

In addition to her personal devotions, she and Jason continued the family devotional time after the evening meal which Jason had begun. They kept the time short, only reading a few verses and praying together, both feeling the family needed the daily time of looking to God together.

Frank was the only family member who seemed uncomfortable with the devotional time. When Pearl asked Jason about Frank's faith, his eyes became troubled. "Mom and Dad always saw to it the family was churchgoing, and made no secret of the fact they believed faith in Christ was the most important part of a person's life. I just assumed Frank had committed his life to Christ, as I did. Afraid I was wrong, considering his actions lately. I tried to talk with him about it, but he just shrugged me off."

They agreed to pray for Frank to come to a realization of his need for Christ. It hurt to see him trying to deal with the changes in his life by leaning on liquor instead of the Lord.

Before long school began and Pearl assumed some of Maggie's duties. The only item which made it easier for Pearl to complete her work was her freedom of time spent watching Grace. Grace turned six in early September and was attending school for the first time. She and Maggie walked the three miles to school in Chippewa City each day.

Grace's school attendance brought the need for new clothes and added another item to Pearl's growing list of duties. Jason brought his mother's sewing machine into the kitchen, where Pearl could work and still be available to answer Maggie's questions as she studied algebra, geography, and natural philosophy at the kitchen table.

As soon as he could be spared from the fields, Andy would be attending classes, also. It had been his father's dream that all of his children graduate and the boys continue their education beyond the traditional eight years of school. It was an unusual dream in a land where few boys graduated. Those who did normally took more than eight years to reach that goal, and Jason and Frank were not exceptions.

One rainy Saturday afternoon when Jason and Andy returned from delivering grain to the elevator, Andy's eyes were as large as wagon wheels. "There were one hundred ponies from Wyoming on First Street! When I'm a man, I'm heading west to be a cowboy."

"I can remember when this *was* the West," Pearl said when Andy left the room.

Jason poured a cup of coffee from the large graniteware pot. "He wanted to join the circus when Oliver's World's Greatest Shows was in town in April."

Leaning against the table, he watched Pearl ironing. "I don't understand Frank anymore. He used to argue with Dad all the time about continuing his education. Said all he ever wanted was to be a farmer and couldn't see any reason to go back to school when he was perfectly happy right here. Now all he talks about is attending Windom Institute." Jason raked a hand through his hair. "Frank wants to become a business man and Andy wants to be a cowboy. Don't know who Dad thought he was building the farm up for."

Pearl placed the cooling iron on the stove to reheat and changed the wooden handle to a hot iron. She watched Jason's back through the window as he walked to the barn. He hadn't wanted the farm, either. Her heart ached for him.

Grace's nightmares added to the family's exhaustion. They were diminishing in quantity but not intensity. Pearl and Jason asked the Lord fervently to show them how to help the poor child.

One Tuesday night in mid-September, a bloodcurdling scream brought Pearl bolt-upright. Almost before she was awake she'd slipped into the flannel wrapper she kept across the foot of her bed.

She collided with Jason in the hallway in front of Grace's door. Corduroy trousers stuck out beneath his night shirt. "I'll see to her. You need your sleep," she offered.

"We'll both take care of her."

It was a conversation they had every night. The result never changed. They stayed up together with the girl until the memory of the nightmare dulled enough for her to go back to sleep.

Pearl led the way downstairs with a lamp and Jason followed carrying the kicking and screaming child. They'd learned from painful and exhausting experience that the screaming wouldn't end for at least a half-hour and it would be a good deal longer before she quieted enough to allow them to leave her and return to bed.

Jason sat in the spring rocker in the parlor, whispering comforting words to the girl in his arms, ignoring the kicks and blows. Seeing the pain and concern for Grace etched deeply into Jason's dry, tanned skin added to the pain Pearl felt for Grace. She sat on the settee, lifting silent prayers for both.

After a long time, the screams subsided into scattered,

wrenching sobs which slowly disappeared into occasional shaky breaths. For the dozenth time, Pearl and Jason urged her to tell them about the dream that frightened her so but as always she was unable to describe it. All she would say was, "I'm 'fwaid you're goin' ta be mad and go away, like Mommy and Papa."

No amount of reassurances would convince her otherwise.

"Do you think your mommy and papa are angry with you, dear?" Pearl asked. Why hadn't she heard that part of Grace's cry before, instead of only hearing that the child was afraid they'd leave her?

She nodded, her wet little face brushing against Jason's flannel robe.

"Why?"

"If they weren't mad, why don't they come home?"

Pearl saw the sheen of tears in Jason's eyes before he bent his head over his sister. His groan ripped through her. "Mommy and Papa aren't staying away because they're mad at you, pumpkin. They can't come home because they're in heaven. Heaven is a wonderful place but people can't leave there."

"Why?"

"I don't know why; I only know they can't."

Pearl swallowed the sob that rose in her own throat at the hopelessness in Jason's husky answer.

"Why did they go there? Don't they love me any more?"

"Of course they do, pumpkin. They love you so much that Pearl and I were given special orders to stay with you and watch over you for them."

A thumb slipped into her mouth as she considered this and she was silent for a minute. "Is special orders like a pwomise?"

Jason's lips stretched in a sad smile. "Yes. It's something we won't ever change our minds about."

"I want to talk to Mommy and Papa," she mumbled around her thumb.

Jason closed his eyes tight but Pearl intervened before he could respond.

"When I was even smaller than you, my mommy died and went to heaven. My brother, Johnny, and I wanted to talk to her, too. Johnny finally came up with a way we could talk to her even though we couldn't see her and she couldn't answer us."

Grace's big brown eyes searched her face for a full minute. "How?"

"When we prayed, we would ask God to give her our messages, and tell her we loved her and missed her."

"Did He do that?"

Pearl forced a bright smile. "Oh, I'm sure He did. God takes very good care of people when they go to heaven."

Grace looked at Jason for confirmation and he nodded. Pearl saw his Adam's apple jerk before he said, "Sure as shootin', pumpkin."

"I'm goin' to ask Him to tell Mommy and Papa I love them."

"Good idea."

They had just tucked her back in bed when Frank's slurred voice raised in song came through the windows.

"Drunk again!" Disgust drenched Jason's whisper.

"Don't argue with him now. You need your sleep. It's less than two hours until sunrise."

"Two hours won't be enough to sleep off that hangover."

"Fall term begins tomorrow at Windom Institute. I expect that's what brought this on in the middle of the week."

"Is that supposed to be an excuse? A man should be able to handle life's disappointments without resorting to the bottle."

"Getting angry won't help anything and will keep you from needed rest."

But he was already heading for the top of the stairs. "I'll have to put up his horse. He never remembers to take care of her when he comes home in this shape."

Pearl couldn't sleep right away when she went back to bed; she kept listening for Jason to return. She didn't mind the heavy work load so much but the emotional tension of dealing with Grace night after night, and the strain of Frank's belligerence and drinking made her weary. She'd told Jason she was meant to be his helpmate but she didn't seem capable of dealing with the things with which he needed help the most. If she found these things wearying, how much more must they affect him?

❧

Pearl stood on the porch the next evening watching Frank herd the milk cows into the barn. Their bawling filled the air. *Complaining of the heat as much as of their full udders,* she thought, wiping the back of her hand over her brow. It would be hotter in the barn but at least they would be free of the sand whipped around by the prairie winds. One hundred degrees in the shade. It certainly didn't feel like the middle of September.

In spite of their heavy work load, the men always milked the cows. Frank was handling the milking today because Jason refused to allow him in the fields because of last night's drinking. Her own work had kept her from even considering helping with the milking in the past. Not that she'd ever milked a cow before but she'd seen it done and it didn't look too hard.

She stuck her head in the kitchen door where Maggie was pumping water at the sink to fill the bedroom water pitchers. "I'm going to the barn. Keep an eye on Grace."

Frank was taking a milk pail down from its peg when she entered the barn, the air thick with the odors of cows and hay. "I've come to help."

Frank shook his head. "Jason wouldn't like that."

She reached for a pail. "Nonsense. Will you teach me or shall I teach myself?"

Grinning, he took the pail from her. "Afraid it's the cows who wouldn't approve of you teaching yourself."

Almost two hours passed before she looked up from the three-legged stool beside a brown and white cow to see Jason looking down at her with a puzzled frown. "Maggie told me I'd find you in here. What are you doing?"

She giggled. "Well, if you can't tell, I'm obviously doing it wrong."

"I don't want you doing the milking."

A shrug lifted the shoulders of her damp blouse and she continued her pulling. "I'm glad to do it. You and your brothers have more than you can handle already."

"You've been working sunup to sundown and beyond yourself, and you don't see me trying to take on any of your work load."

The cow's tail hit her full in the face. Pearl sputtered and shook her head. "It's not the same thing."

He grinned and grabbed the cow's tail to keep it from striking her again. "It's just the same thing. I don't want you doing this."

"But I like helping you."

"Let me finish." He took her arm just above the wrist and gently tugged.

"Ouch!"

In a second he was kneeling in the straw beside her, holding her arm between his callused hands more gently than she would have believed possible. "Your wrists are swollen!"

He touched his lips to them and her breath caught in a light gasp at the sweet, spontaneous gesture. "They. . .they're fine, truly. I just didn't realize milking was so hard."

He kept her arm in his hands as he turned his gaze to hers.

The corners of his mouth tipped up. "Did I actually hear you admit there's something a man can do better than a woman? After all the times you told John and me that you could do anything we could do?"

"I didn't say a man could do it better; I only said it's hard. My muscles will become accustomed to it."

He stood, pulling her up with him. "No, they won't. You aren't to do it again."

It was the first time he'd given her an order. An order it definitely was, in spite of his tender tone.

When she opened her mouth to protest, he laid his fingers over her lips. "I spend all day in the field and around animals, until I can smell them in my sleep. I don't want my wife to smell like cows."

The gentleness in his eyes stilled any further protest. "I only meant to help. You've been so tired lately."

His hand cupped her chin lightly, his thumb tracing her cheekbone. She trembled at his touch. "You are so sweet." His husky whisper sent goose bumps down her spine. He was so close. Was he. . .was he going to kiss her?

"So what do you think of her first day's milking?"

Jason and Pearl jerked apart at Frank's voice. Jason frowned at him. "Was it you who taught her how to do this?"

Frank leaned against the stall and raised his eyebrows at Pearl. "Told you he wouldn't like it."

"You're right, I don't."

The coldness in his voice had the effect on Pearl of being dumped in ice water. "You needn't bellow at him. It was my idea."

He stepped around her and dropped down on the stool. "Well, I'm taking over now."

"Yes, so I see." She grasped her skirt to keep it from tripping her in the straw and hurried out of the barn. Whatever had she done to change his attitude so suddenly? Everything was wonderful, and then. . . .

"Why do I keep forgetting, Lord?" she asked through clenched teeth, her shoes hitting the hard soil of the yard sharply with each step. "When am I going to learn not to read love into each kind word and look Jason gives me?"

Jason barely noticed the white streams hissing into the pail. His heart felt like someone had plucked it out of his chest and stomped on it. He'd been so touched that Pearl wanted to spare him. In another moment he would have kissed her, told her that he loved her.

Then Frank had spoken and the thought flashed through his mind that perhaps she had done this not to spare him further work but to help Frank.

She'd pleaded Frank's case to him last night, when he'd expected her to be as disgusted with the man as he was himself. She knew Frank had the responsibility for milking tonight. It was him she was assisting, not her husband.

Before they were married, when he and Frank had argued over escorting her home, she'd said she'd always enjoyed Frank's company. It was no secret his brother was considered wildly attractive by most of the single women in town, in spite of the fact he barely said hello to them. He wasn't shy with Pearl. He was as comfortable with her as he was with Maggie. *What if Pearl. . .?*

"No!"

The cow turned her head to look at him and he patted her flank. "Sorry, Bessie. Wasn't yelling at you."

He picked up the pail and walked slowly across the barn, dreading going inside and facing Pearl.

Leaning against the barn door, he listened to piano music from the open windows mix with the music of the prairie insects and allowed the thought he'd stamped out a minute earlier to wriggle inside his mind in all its ugliness.

What if his wife was falling in love with his brother?

twelve

Pearl returned smiles and greetings as she moved down the aisle of Windom Institute's recitation hall joining the rest of the audience during the intermission of the musicale.

She was glad to see it so well attended. With the economic depression, the school was having difficulty meeting its debts, the same as everyone else. Male students had offered to provide the labor required for a much-needed well but the funds from the musicale would purchase the necessary supplies for the well and windmill.

"I'll be back in a minute," Jason said in her ear.

She felt absurdly lonely watching him move through the crowd to stop beside Amy Henderson. Always in public he played the devoted husband and she cherished his touch at her elbow or back and his endearing looks, even knowing they were only for show. The first few days and weeks of their marriage she'd wondered if he could possibly be falling in love with her. He was so sweet and the way he would look at her sometimes—well, even now it made her heart skip a beat. But since the episode in the barn, he'd not touched her in their home unless it was accidental. He remained friendly and even joked as always but there was a definite cooling in his attitude. She was at a loss to understand it.

Amy and Jason parted, and she watched for him to return to her. Jealousy burned through her when Miranda stopped him with a gloved hand on his arm, darting a triumphant look at Pearl.

She turned decidedly away. What right had she to be jealous? She knew when she married him that he loved Miranda.

The knowledge did nothing to decrease her pain.

How had Miranda become so self-centered, she wondered for the hundredth time. With all the unmarried women today seeking employment, her desire for a life of leisure was particularly unseemly. Even Chippewa City was filled with women working beside men—proprietresses of boarding houses and hotels, waitresses, maids, milliners, seamstresses, clerks, secretaries serving the professional men, instructors in music, school teachers, even a banker. Look at the wife of the Windom Institute's headmaster—why, she taught, acted as housemother to the young women boarding there, and cooked for twenty to forty teachers and students daily! If a woman hadn't a family to care for, the world certainly had plenty of places for her to fill a need.

Restlessly, she moved toward a painting on the wall, one of many in an exhibit by Amy. Frank was in a group of young men nearby, she noticed, discoursing on the need for area farmers to support the new grain house in town, which had already advanced the local market two cents above list.

"It's so good to see you again, Mrs. Sterling. You don't get into town nearly often enough." Pearl started at Amy's gentle voice.

She gave Amy an impulsive hug. "You're right. We must get together soon." Would her bright smile fool her friend, she wondered as she waved a hand toward the paintings. "Your work is wonderful. I understand your showing at the Minnesota Exhibition this fall went well?"

"Yes, thank you."

"We're all so proud of you."

With her typical modesty, she changed the subject from her own success. "And you? I do hope you are happy as a married woman."

As happy as she had any right to be, she thought, wedding a man she knew loved another. "I wouldn't give up life with

Jason for anything under the sun." At least that was true.

Amy's smile was warm. "I'm so glad. He is a fine man."

"Are you still seeing Mr. Ray?"

"Occasionally."

Had Amy hesitated before replying? Pearl hoped that meant she had reservations about the man.

"I. . .I hate to give credit to gossip. . ." Amy stopped as though reconsidering, a frown touching her otherwise smooth forehead beneath upswept hair. "I wouldn't even mention it if we weren't close friends."

Pearl laid a hand on Amy's green velvet cape. "What is it?"

"Is it true that Frank has taken up drinking?"

"Yes."

Amy's gaze dropped to her gloved fingers, playing restlessly with the gold braid on her coat. "I was hoping the rumors were false. My contact with Frank has always left me with a favorable opinion of him."

"We'd appreciate your prayers for him."

"You will most certainly have them."

Jason stepped up beside Pearl and took her elbow, his touch causing her pulse to race, as always. "And just what are you giving my wife?"

Pearl looked up at his laughing eyes and felt life drain from her soul. Such a pleased expression hadn't passed his face in weeks. *Were those few minutes with Miranda responsible for it?* She hoped her answering smile wasn't the miserable failure it felt to be. "You've misunderstood Amy's comment," she said as Frank joined them. "We were discussing the need for the women of Chippewa City to pray for the community's wild young men."

Frank's dark eyes grew almost black at her comment but Jason just chuckled. "When it comes to taming men, it takes a powerful dose of prayer."

Amy's delicate chin lifted slightly. "The unmarried members of the Women's Christian Temperance Union here are considering adopting the vow of the young women of nearby Madison. They have banded together in a vow to boycott young men who use tobacco. We would add to it those young men who use intoxicating liquors or frequent billiard halls."

Pearl noticed Amy's gaze rested fully on Frank as she spoke. Frank's lips spread in an uncompromising grimace in spite of the fact that Amy's voice was strictly conversational.

Jason didn't seem to notice the tension between the two. "I should think that would get the men's attention, if anything will." His smile settled into normal proportions. "There's been a lot of talk around town that the drinking is getting out of hand, what with the number of horse and buggy accidents drunkards have had recently not to mention injuries from saloon scuffles."

"Rev. Conrad is encouraging the townspeople to hold socials in their homes for the young people, hoping to keep them from less dangerous pursuits."

The delicate ringing of a hand bell interrupted Amy as a male Institute student walked by indicating the end of the intermission.

Pearl settled gracefully into her chair between Jason and Frank. Rev. Conrad's wife—Aunt Millicent—and Boston had often spoken of fighting against liquor licenses when the town was young. It seemed every generation had to fight the battle for high ideals all over again.

Frank leaned close to whisper, "Miss Amy's sweet voice and manner make her Temperance ideas a might more palatable than when presented by some of her more forceful counterparts. I wonder if she'd feel so strongly if she knew that her precious Ed Ray enjoys his 'intoxicating liquors' as much as the next man—and that's one of his better habits. Why can't a woman see a man for what he is?"

Her gaze darted to him in surprise, but he'd turned back to the stage where the musicale was about to resume. Always when he spoke of Ed Ray, bitterness clogged his voice. *Did he dislike the man so or was it that he cared for Amy?*

Jason's hand closed over hers and her heart dove to her stomach. She stared at the stage, hoping he didn't notice the way his touch had set her trembling. Slowly she turned her head just enough to see his face. He was grinning at her as though he was the proverbial cat that caught the canary. The same pleased look he'd worn after speaking to Miranda. *Was his former fiancée's effect so strong that it would last the entire evening?*

She turned her attention back to the stage and did something she'd never done before. Gently but deliberately, she extricated her hand from his.

❧

Jason set the lamp he'd carried downstairs with him on the kitchen table. The room seemed warm after the unheated bedroom. Even so, he was glad he'd dressed. No sense trying to sleep any longer. Between worrying about Frank and thinking about Pearl, he'd been awake all night. Must be two o'clock by now.

He sat down heavily beside the table and rested his head in his hands. Would Frank get home before dawn? *I shouldn't have let him go sleighing with his Institute friends after the musicale,* Jason thought. He snorted. *Stupid thought.* Frank was eighteen; how could he have prevented him from going?

Besides, Jason admitted reluctantly, he'd been eager to be alone with Pearl on the sleigh ride home. He'd had such hopes for tonight and it had been a disaster from beginning to end. It was the first time they'd been out together since their wedding and he'd entertained the thought that perhaps it would be a new start for them.

He'd about convinced himself he'd let his imagination get

away from him, thinking his wife was attracted to his brother. He'd stomped out of his memory the dozens of times he saw them together laughing or talking in this very room.

Was there any way after tonight that a reasonable man could believe anything but that his wife preferred his brother's company to his own?

When she'd turned from whispering with Frank to coldly draw her hand from his, the pain was so great he'd wished his heart would simply stop beating.

Immediately before that, he'd been thinking of the pleasure his gift would give her. Amy had agreed to do a painting for Pearl for Christmas and he couldn't stop grinning from that moment until Pearl so uncharacteristically pulled away from him. Even Miranda's embarrassing flirtation hadn't taken away the joy of arranging something special for Pearl. It shamed him to think he could ever have cared for a woman who would behave so brazenly as Miranda did tonight toward a married man.

His groan seemed to echo off the walls. Pearl gave unstintingly of herself to him and his family, never complaining, never refusing anyone. His love for her grew with every passing day, with her every act of kindness.

He never thought when he asked her to marry him that he might be stealing from her the opportunity to spend her life with a man she loved. He only knew he wanted her in his life and was sure God would bring her around to loving him.

True, he'd been grieving, had lost so much in a short time that his heart cried out for a loving and loyal touch. He knew better than to think that justified what he'd done. He hadn't been thinking of Pearl's needs at all when he proposed, only his own. Love wasn't like that—selfish and grasping. It was giving, like Pearl.

The clear jangle of bells came through the still air, breaking into his thoughts. Jason scraped back his chair and hurried to the window. By the light of the lanterns on the sleigh, he could see Frank all but fall from the cutter. The driver laughed, turned the horse about and headed down the drive.

The sky had been clear earlier in the evening, a nice night for a sleigh drive. It was snowing now and the wind was coming up. Relief flooded him that Frank had arrived home safe. The prairie during a snowy night was no place for a drunken man.

He opened the door and helped Frank inside, screwing up his face at the liquor odor that hung strongly about his brother.

Frank leaned heavily against him and hiccuped. "Howdy, big brother."

"Let's take off your coat and boots and get you to bed."

"Don't want ta go ta bed!" Frank pulled away from his hold, stumbling against the table.

Jason grabbed the lamp as it started to tilt. "Watch it!"

Frank's lips spread in a grin. "Don't need ta watch anythin'. You do all the watchin' fer both of us."

"You're drunk."

Frank waved his index finger back and forth in front of his face then began following the motion with his head. "Yup. Big brother takes care of all of us, whether we want him to or not."

Jason tried to take his arm again but he dodged. "Someone has to watch out for you when you're drunk like this."

"I kin watch out fer myself."

"Oh? You can't even talk straight, let alone walk or think straight. Isn't it about time you sobered up and started acting like a man?"

Frank weaved closer to him and his breath smelled like spoiled yeast as he laughed in Jason's face. "That's funny, you tellin' me ta act like a man." He leaned heavily on Jason's shoulder. "You treat yer wife like a hired girl. Least I'm man enough ta expect ta share my wife's bed when I marry."

Fury poured through his veins like molten rock. He pushed Frank from him.

"Jason, don't!"

Pearl's scream reached him as Frank landed against the door with a sickening thud. He ignored her and jerked his brother up by the lapels of his woolen coat. "How dare you insult my wife that way?"

"Jason!" Pearl's hands clung to his arm and he felt all her weight straining to pull him away.

He glanced at her to tell her to let go but the fright in her eyes stopped him.

"I won't have you fighting with your brother over me."

With a growl, he dropped his brother's lapels and Frank fell back against the door. Jason watched as he picked himself up and stumbled outside.

Jason's breath was coming as fast as a horse's after a quarter-mile gallop. "You wouldn't have defended him if you heard what he said. He was only speaking the truth."

He clenched his fists at his sides, trying to ease the rage and pain inside him.

Her bottom lip trembled slightly and she caught it between her teeth. She brushed back the hair that fell waist-length over her shoulders, kinked from the braids that held it earlier. Her voice was soft and controlled when she continued, "How can he be expected to understand our unusual marriage? Have you explained it to him?"

Tell his brother he'd married a woman who didn't love him? "No." He all but hollered the word.

The pain in her eyes lanced through him. One hand closed on her shoulder. "Pearl. . . ."

The wind howled around the corners of the house and whistled between the door and frame, pouring cold air over him. The chill sent slivers of terror through him. *How long had the wind been blowing like that?*

He swung open the door, only to close it quickly against the snow that swirled over the threshold. He stuffed his feet into the boots beside the door. "Better make some coffee."

"Where are you going?"

"To find Frank. A storm's coming up." Pulling on his jacket he asked, "Is there a lantern in here?"

When she returned from the pantry a minute later with a rope, lantern, and matches, he was tying a muffler over his hat and around his throat.

His hand hesitated over hers on the handle of the lantern. At the sight of the terror in her face, his anger melted away. She was trying valiantly to hide her fear but he'd known her too long and too well to be deceived. He couldn't bear her hurting so, even if it was for love of his brother.

His free hand cupped the back of her neck and pulled her against his jacket. "Don't worry," he whispered gruffly against her hair. "I'll find him. Likely he's in the barn, sleeping it off."

A moment later he plunged into the wintery night.

thirteen

Jason pushed his shoulder against the kitchen door two hours later, shutting out the storm. It took all his strength. He leaned against the door, trying to catch his breath. His muscles felt like he'd been pushing mountains around instead of wind and snow.

His eyelids closed. He let them stay that way, ice-coated lashes resting on his numb cheeks. How was he going to tell Pearl he hadn't found Frank? Maybe he wouldn't have to; maybe Frank had come home himself.

"Jason! Thank God!"

He knew the minute he saw her face that his brother was still out in the storm.

Pearl's fingers tugged at the ice-covered knot of the rope around his waist.

"I didn't find him."

"I know." One of her fingernails snapped and he saw her cringe but she didn't stop working at the knot. "You need to get into something dry."

"I didn't want to quit looking, to leave him out there, but I couldn't see more than a couple inches in front of me and. . . ."

"I know, dear. You did everything you could." She began to make progress with the knot. A minute later she had it undone. "Get out of these wet things. I'll bring you some dry clothes."

She busied herself at the stove while he changed, keeping her back to him, then urged him into the sturdy oak rocking chair beside the stove.

She'd changed while he was out, into a simple flannel house gown that reminded him of the rich color of a blue jay's feathers. He liked the way it deepened the color of her eyes.

He had to force his fingers to hold the cup of coffee she handed him. They were still stiff and red, and burning from the cold. His feet were the same but Pearl had heated the brick used in the buggy and his feet sat warming upon it now. When she tucked a thick quilt over his lap, he wanted to pull her down on top of it and let their arms comfort each other.

Pearl knelt by his chair and took one of his hands in hers. Laying her cheek against it, she whispered brokenly, "Let's pray together for him."

His words of prayer came haltingly. It seemed he'd been praying the entire time he was searching but to say the words out loud made the knowledge that Frank's life was completely out of his hands all too real. It didn't help knowing that if he hadn't blown up at his brother when he was drunk, Frank would be safe asleep upstairs right now.

He set the coffee mug on the stove beside him and laid his hand on Pearl's head where it rested on his knee. The stinging of the receding numbness in his body was insignificant beside the longing to take her pain on himself. "I'm sorry, Pearl."

"For what?" Puzzlement shone in her eyes.

"For arguing with him, forcing him out into the storm."

"You didn't force him to do anything. Frank is a man. He makes his own choices, even if they aren't wise."

He wished he could believe her. If Frank didn't make it—well, he wouldn't allow himself to think about that now. As long as there was a chance Frank was alive, he wouldn't give up hope.

Pearl rubbed his hand briskly between her own. "Drink your coffee. You need the warmth." She pushed to her feet and headed toward the freestanding cupboard which held the ironstone dishes. "I made some oatmeal while you were out, too. It won't be as good as if it had steamed all night but it's nourishing."

"Thanks, but I'm not hungry." *Not for food, anyway.* He wished he dared ask her to come back and simply sit holding his hand again.

"You haven't stopped shivering since you came inside." She handed him a steaming bowl. "Now eat this."

He smiled meekly as he accepted it, the effort cracking his chapped lips. "Yes, Nurse." He ate the oatmeal faithfully as she busied herself about the kitchen, setting the table for breakfast, then covering it with a cloth trimmed in red. He knew she was only trying to keep her mind as occupied as possible.

Likely she was constantly pushing away the picture of Frank lying somewhere with the snow piling over him, the same as he was. Silently he repeated the prayer for Frank's safety.

When he finished the oatmeal, she took the bowl from him. He caught her hand, and she stopped, looking down at him with a question in her eyes.

"I'm sorry. About the argument earlier, I mean." He didn't ever want to argue with her again. When he was out in the storm, two thoughts kept battling each other: the need to find Frank, and the regret that he and Pearl had parted angry.

His thumb played across the back of her hand and he felt her fingers tighten around his. Unable to look her in the eyes, he watched their hands instead. "Was Frank right? Do you feel like a hired girl?"

The lamplight glinted off her long blond hair as she shook her head. "No. I don't mind the work. I'm your helpmate, remember?"

She'd avoided the real question but he let it pass. "Are you sorry you married me?" The words seemed to scratch his throat. His heartbeat throbbed in his ears. If only he could catch the words back! What if she said yes?

"No, only. . . ."

He swallowed the lump in his throat. "Only what?"

Her lashes dropped and were framed against her cheek. It gave her a demure, vulnerable look he wasn't accustomed to seeing in her and did funny things to his heart.

"Only sometimes I'm afraid our marriage has ruined our friendship. You were always the dearest, most fun comrade," she rushed on as though eager to explain, lifting her lashes and looking earnestly into his eyes, "but now you so often draw away from me and seem almost angry." She took a shaky breath. "Are. . .are you sorry you married me?"

Was he? Yes, if she loved Frank. But sorry to have her here in his home, beside him every day? "No. No, I'm not sorry. I miss the close friendship we shared, too. How about if we make a pact to get it back?"

Her smile was brilliant. "I'd like that." She moved toward the pantry. "You need some glycerin for your chapped lips and hands."

The lamp on the table cast only a dim, mellow light in that part of the kitchen. Maybe that made it easier to ask. "Why did you agree to marry me?"

She stopped moving for a full ten seconds. Would she ignore the question? "You said you needed me."

It wasn't the answer he longed to hear but he hadn't any choice but to accept it.

"I love being part of your family. Some moments I almost feel like a mother to the younger ones." She wrapped her arms over her chest and he had the fleeting thought that she was trying to comfort herself. "Being here has made me wonder about my own mother—the one who died. I didn't think I remembered her well enough to miss her until I came here. Now I wonder whether she'd wanted to move here—to what was then the frontier, whether she loved my father, what her dreams were for Johnny and me, what she thought and feared and prayed for concerning us when she knew she was going to die and had to leave us."

"I've been wondering some of the same things about my own mother these last few months." He cleared the huskiness from his throat and reached a hand to her. "Come here."

Did his request sound as much like begging to her as it did to him?

She took his hand hesitantly and he tugged gently. "Come here," he repeated softly.

He pulled her into his lap, cradling her in his arms, rejoicing in the feel of her head resting against his shoulder, even as he ached for her pain. Teardrops glistened on her lashes but she didn't cry. He couldn't recall ever seeing her cry. If only his arms wrapped around her could draw her pain away!

One hand cupped the back of her head and slid down the length of golden hair. Never had he felt anything so silky. The only time he saw her hair down was during Grace's nightmares. It had been years since she'd worn it down in public. A tremor ran through her at his touch and he regretfully forced his hands to be still.

Tentatively, he rested his cheek against her hair. He'd wanted to give her comfort and instead he was frightening her. "Dear Lord, we thank Thee for Pearl's parents and the love they must have had for the little girl they had to entrust into Thy care after having her with them for such a short time. Thank Thee for the hopes and prayers they had for Pearl, which are known only unto Thee. And for Doctor Matt and Boston, who love her as their own. In Thy Son's name, Amen."

"Oh, Jason!" Her words were a half-sob that wrenched his heart.

"I wish I could take away all your pain," he whispered hoarsely.

"And I yours."

At a noise from the floor above them, Pearl pushed herself quickly from his lap. "I'd best get breakfast. Andy and the girls will be rising soon."

Regret swept over him. Perhaps it was for the best. It had become more difficult every moment to keep from lifting her face to his and kissing her the way he'd longed to do for months.

"The kids all love you. Maggie thinks the sun rises and sets with you. And Grace—thanks to you, her nightmares are almost a thing of the past. The scrapbook you started for her was an inspiration, asking each of us to write down a memory of things Mom and Dad did that showed how much they loved her and then letting her draw pictures in the book to illustrate them. It's become her favorite storybook."

"It's your family's love that healed her. Love is stronger than any fear."

"Yes, I suppose it is." Gratitude for the blessing she was to his family warmed his soul. She'd given so much to all of them. For them it was worth the constant fire that raged inside him, the continual yearning for her love, regardless if she ever returned his affection. But for her? "You've been a great helpmate these last few months. I've sure made a mess of being the head of this family."

"That's not true. You've kept everyone together, kept the farm running, made the payments on your father's bank note, seen to it there was food on the table, and that all the family's needs have been met."

Sausage sizzled in a pan, its odor covering that of the kerosene lamp and the fire in the stove.

He propped his elbows on the rocker's oaken arms and clasped his hands together in front of him. "I've alienated Frank somehow. Can't understand his drinking and carousing and temper tantrums. He never used to do such things."

"Perhaps he's trying to find a way to deal with his grief."

"I would have sworn he knew better than to think a man could handle his problems that way." He ran a hand through his unkempt hair. "Sometimes I want to ask him to leave home and support himself. Maybe that would make him sober up and act responsibly. But the farm and house are as much his as mine, and I've no right to demand he leave."

"Remember your mother's sampler? 'Charity hopeth all things.' We need to keep believing in Frank and hoping for him, Jason. Eventually God will show you a way to make peace with him."

If he's still alive. He pushed the thought from his mind. "Our God is the God of hope." Her smile warmed some of the ice around his heart.

The God of hope. The thought cheered him. Maybe God would see to getting Frank back in the right path. And maybe He'd even bring Pearl around to loving him. Maybe. The flame of hope he'd thought extinguished began to flicker once more.

"Is. . .is there any chance Frank might be able to go to Windom Institute for winter term?"

Arguing Frank's cause again! His heart constricted painfully. He wasn't about to remind her that the arguments might be meaningless if Frank. . . . He swallowed, not allowing himself to complete the thought.

"Do you think giving in to him on Windom would stop his drinking? Even if it did, wouldn't he only resort to drinking again when he runs into life's next disappointment?"

"I wasn't thinking only of his drinking. I was thinking. . ." she hesitated, then rushed on, "I have so much admiration for you and your willingness to sacrifice for your family. Of course, I never thought for a moment you would do anything less, but. . . ."

"Forget the flattery. What is the 'but'?"

"Perhaps God isn't asking the same sacrifices of Frank that He's asking of you."

It hadn't once occurred to him to ask God whether he should support Frank's wish to go to Windom this year. All this time, he'd thought he was relying on God's strength to run the farm and keep the family together. Had he been kidding himself—only been relying on God to help him go his own way?

"I'll pray about it," came Jason's hoarse response.

fourteen

The storm buffeted the house all the next day. The Sterling family even had to keep lamps lit because of the heavy snow and cloud cover.

But the quiet among the family was more stifling than the darkness or the howling wind. Everyone but Grace was painfully aware of the dangers of a prairie blizzard. Only five years earlier the infamous blizzard of '88 had claimed many lives across the upper plains states, including the lives of some of their neighbors.

After Jason had explained the situation to Maggie and Andrew, no one had spoken of it. They all realized that until the wind died down there was nothing any of them could do but pray. By unspoken agreement they kept busy with work about the house, homework, or playing with Grace. Every few minutes someone would go to stand beside a window, or put on a coat and walk out on the porch, vainly seeking for a moving figure in the blinding snow.

Jason and Andrew tied ropes around their waists and went to the barn to care for the animals and chickens. The temperature had dropped drastically and Pearl felt sorry for the creatures. Their water would likely be frozen before they had a chance to drink more than a few swallows.

When they returned from the barn, Jason noticed Pearl had moved the sampler that had hung in his parents' bedroom to the wall above the kitchen table. A silent reminder not to give up on Frank.

The storm still blew that night and it was almost morning before it calmed. Immediately after breakfast, Andrew and

Jason put on snowshoes and began to search again for Frank. Maggie left for neighboring farms to inquire if anyone had seen Frank, and to request assistance in the search. For once Jason allowed Pearl to care for the cows and chickens.

It was still early when Jason, Andrew, and Maggie returned with Frank. The relief at finding him alive filled all their faces.

It turned out Frank had lost his way in the storm, eventually stumbling against Thor Lindstrom's barn. Realizing it would be suicide to try to leave the building, he'd huddled in the hay beneath a horse blanket. Thor found him there the next morning when he worked his way to the barn with a rope around his waist to care for the animals. Frank knew his family would be worried sick about him, but there was nothing to be done but stay with Thor and Ellie until the storm wore itself out.

He'd set out this morning with Thor accompanying him. The good-hearted Scandinavian wanted to make certain Frank had the strength to make it home. On the way, they'd met the Sterlings. Pearl never heard whether any cross words were spoken between Frank and Jason at that meeting. She only knew that relief eased the lines of fatigue and fear that had been etched in Jason's face during the prior thirty-six hours and her heart rejoiced with thanksgiving to God.

Two apple pies filled the kitchen with their delectable odor as Pearl pulled them from the oven a few hours later, reflecting on how quickly the household had settled back to normal. Finding Frank so quickly and finding him healthy had almost been anticlimactic.

Jason and Andrew were now busy clearing a path from the house to the barn. That and clearing an area in the corral and in front of the chicken coop would take them most of the afternoon. A few minutes earlier, Maggie had taken a restless Grace outside to make a snow man. The little girl's happy squeals could be heard through the closed windows.

"Guess I caused a mess of trouble, huh?"

She set the pies carefully on the wooden rack on the free-standing cupboard and looked over at Frank. The dark, deep-set eyes that so many Chippewa City misses found romantic were watching her broodingly.

"It's behind us. We're all just glad you're back safe and sound." *Would this experience convince him to stop drinking?* She fervently hoped so.

"I owe you an apology."

She lifted the cover of the Dutch oven on the stove top. The tantalizing scent of beef stew drifted into the room. "Oh?"

"For saying those things about you and Jason the other night."

She hoped he'd think it was the heat of the stove coloring her face.

A chapped hand brushed back his black hair impatiently. "I don't understand. You know more than anyone how much Jason loved Miranda. Why did you marry him?"

"I love him." She could hardly believe the calm with which she met his challenging look. The seconds grew long as they stared. She refused to look away first, as though loving Jason was something of which to be ashamed.

His hands plunged into his pockets. "I know what it's like to love someone who cares for another. Seems I've loved Amy Henderson since I first began noticing girls."

Frank in love with Amy!

He cleared his throat. "Appreciate it if you wouldn't mention it to anyone. Haven't even told Jason."

There were biscuits to be made for dinner but she didn't move. It wasn't easy for him to confess his love for Amy and she didn't want to show disrespect for his admission.

"Why haven't you courted her?"

He snorted. Anger filled the eyes he turned to her, making

them look black. "Think she'd be interested in a farmer when the almighty Ed Ray, a man planning to be a lawyer, is courting her? If I'd ever entertained such a foolish notion, Miranda's refusal to marry Jason would have killed it."

"You do Amy a disservice, comparing her to Miranda. It's not a man's vocation that will win Amy's love; it's a man's character."

"Ed Ray hasn't a shred of character! Why are women so blind? Why can't she see that Ed's everything she says she detests? He can drink me under the table in no time."

"You needn't growl about it. The truth about a man's character always comes out in time."

"Hope it's before she marries the louse."

Pearl measured the flour into a sieve. "Is that why you want to go to Windom Institute? To impress Amy?"

She'd added soda, cream of tartar, salt, and sugar, and ran the mixture through the sieve before he answered. "Yes. Sounds downright stupid when you put it into words like that."

"She'd be more impressed if you quit drinking. At the musicale, she told me she was upset you'd turned to it."

Surprise flickered in his eyes. "She did?"

"Yes. She thought it a shame such a fine young man was acquiring such a destructive habit."

Hands on the oilcloth table covering, he leaned across to look into her face. "She called me a fine young man?"

"Yes." She didn't try to hide the twinkle in her eyes. "I give you fair warning, she's praying that you'll give up drinking."

"It would be worth it, for Amy."

His vehemence was almost convincing but Jason's comment cut through her memory. If he gave up drinking for Amy, would he only return to it again the next time something difficult happened in his life?

She rolled out the dough and reached for the tin biscuit

cutter. "There are many men who don't drink. While that's important to Amy, it isn't enough in itself to win her love."

"And what is?"

"A God-fearing man. A man with enough character to do what's right for no other reason but that it *is* right, regardless of the consequences."

With a mutter she couldn't decipher, he turned his back.

"If you want to go to Windom Institute so badly, why have you stayed on the farm? Why haven't you tried to find a position to earn the money to pay tuition?"

He jammed his hands into his pockets and walked to the window. "Jason and Andrew would have had to hire another man to help with the harvest and threshing. That would more than double the expense of my tuition. It wouldn't be fair to the family."

So he felt the burden of the family the same as Jason. "Amy would approve of that aspect of your character. So do I."

A flush spread over his high cheekbones. "I've already destroyed any chance I might have had with Amy. She'd never consider courting me, with my drinking and all."

"You can change. God doesn't give up on us because we make mistakes. If we ask Him to forgive us and help us change, He meets us where we are and gives us a new start. God's love couldn't hope all things for us without that and we couldn't hope all things for each other."

He slouched against the window frame. "Once I had all kinds of dreams for the future. I don't believe in fairy tales any more."

She placed the biscuits in the oven. "Dreams seldom fall into our lives like gifts all wrapped up in fancy bows. Hopes and dreams require effort; we must live like we believe they will happen.

"You're a farmer. You know you don't have a crop without plowing and planting and caring for the crops while they're growing. You can't make hopes and dreams happen any more than a farmer can make grain grow from a seed—only God can do that. But we can kill hope by not nurturing it, as a farmer can his crops."

Scorn curled his lips. "You're living in a rainbow world." His arm shot toward the window. "See that? It's winter—cold and barren and hard, just like life."

"Spring and summer and fall, with all their beauty, warmth, and abundant life are just as real as winter. Life doesn't stay hard forever."

He swung from the window, his eyes burning into hers. "Doesn't it?" he demanded. "How easy will life be for you, living out your years with a man who loves another woman?"

fifteen

*How easy will life be for you, living out your years with a
man who loves another woman?* Pearl rubbed her fingers
against her temples, wishing she could rub Frank's words
from her mind. His challenge had been slipping into her
thoughts at least once every waking hour for the last week,
taunting her faith.

"I won't believe Jason will never love me," she whispered
fiercely. "I won't!"

She pulled a linen tablecloth for tomorrow's Thanksgiving
dinner from the hope chest that sat at the end of her bed.
Sinking down on top of the chest, she rubbed a hand along
the smooth finish. Dr. Matt and Boston had given the chest
to her for Christmas one year. She'd always loved it.

*How silly to think something as intangible as hope could
be kept in a chest!*

She stood and strode swiftly to the door. Paused. Or was it
silly? Was making and storing things for the day one would
marry a way of making hope real, helping it grow, keeping it
alive—as she'd told Frank one must do?

Of course, one couldn't hope for just anything and expect
God to produce it. But if the desired object is God's will—
such as husbands and wives loving each other—could it be
wrong to encourage that hope?

A picture flashed in her mind—a picture of herself filling
the hope chest with acts of love for Jason. She'd call that
picture to mind to replace Frank's ugly words whenever they
assailed her.

❧

Warmth wrapped around Jason's heart as he looked down the long table to where Pearl sat at the other end. This was the way it should be, the two of them surrounded by happy family. All the leaves had been added to the dining room table to accommodate the guests: Dr. Matt, Boston, Johnny, Jewell, and curly-haired Billy. Having Pearl's family with them for the first holiday since his parents died made it easier for him and his brothers and sisters.

The kitchen had been busy as a beehive all day with the women chattering away while making all the traditional Thanksgiving foods. The smell of roasting turkey had filled the house, and brought the men to the kitchen time and again hoping for something to satisfy their tempted appetites.

"Would anyone like another piece of pumpkin pie?" Pearl asked.

"Sara doesn't have any pie." Grace giggled at her own humor, her large brown eyes spilling over with laughter.

Everyone smiled at her enjoyment of her joke. Only two months old, Johnny and Jewell's little Sara wouldn't be having any pie this Thanksgiving Day.

"No more pie for me. I'm going to have my hands full." Jason reached into the basket setting between him and Jewell, and lifted the sleeping baby. How could anything be so fragile, he wondered, laying Sara gently against his shoulder. The feel of her trusting, tiny body against his chest created a yearning in the pit of his stomach.

Pearl set a piece of pie on Jewell's plate and smiled down at him, shaking her head. "Couldn't even wait until the child awoke."

Did Jason imagine it or were her eyes misty? "Some temptations are impossible to resist."

"You can say that again. I never get my fill of holding her." Johnny grinned. "Maybe you'll have one of your own soon."

Pearl's gaze darted away from Jason's as though burned. He watched her continue dishing out pie. *What was she thinking?* "When we have our own," he replied softly, "I want to start just like you did, with a girl. A little replica of her mother."

Pearl's eyes flashed a surprised look at him. She turned away quickly but not before he'd seen the pain in her face and felt it sear through him. He hadn't intended to hurt her.

Did she think she would never have her own children? The thought almost stopped his heart. *Did she think she'd sacrificed that dream when she agreed to marry him?*

He rubbed his chin lightly against Sara's sweet-smelling head. Pearl's daughter; what an incredible gift that would be.

While the adults had a cup of coffee "to settle their meal," conversation covered a myriad of topics: the continuing political argument regarding silver versus other currencies, reports of the growing number of unemployed men across the nation, the effect of the depression on Chippewa City where "hard times" prices were becoming normal and sales were primarily for cash, the recent fire at the local mill—thought to be incendiary, and last week's blizzard—in which a local woman died walking to her in-laws' farm.

Jason's gaze flew to Frank and his throat suddenly felt thick. Seventy-five-mile-an-hour winds when Frank was out in that blizzard! *Thank You, Lord, for saving him.*

Maggie, Andrew, and Billy told of being sent home from school earlier in the week because the building was so cold that the ink was freezing in the ink wells, and of kids bringing their mothers' spoons and knives to plate silver in natural philosophy class, and of teachers requiring whisperers in class to memorize portions of the Constitution.

Dr. Matt leaned back in his chair, hooked one thumb under the lapel of his coat, adjusted the silver-edged spectacles he always wore now and told about the trip to the World's Exhibition in Chicago.

"Why don't we all tell something for which we're especially thankful this year?" Mother Boston suggested during a lull.

Jason's lips pressed a kiss on the top of Sara's head and he winked at Johnny. "Bet I know what you and Jewell are most thankful for this Thanksgiving."

Johnny laughed and squeezed Jewell's hand. "Bet your guess is right."

"I'm most thankful that Pearl married Jason and came to live with us," Maggie volunteered.

"Me, too." Did Jason's voice sound as gravely to everyone else as it did to him?

Pearl smiled at Maggie, avoiding Jason's eyes. Had he angered her? Things had been so good between them again since the night of the storm. He couldn't go back to the tension they'd endured before. He wouldn't. He noticed Boston lift her eyebrows inquiringly at Pearl and the almost imperceptible answering shake of Pearl's head. What was that all about?

Frank scraped back his chair and threw down his napkin. "Far as I can see, Pearl's the only good thing that's happened to this family all year."

Jason's jaw was rigid in his effort to control his anger as Frank stormed from the room. He knew better than to act like that in front of company!

"Please excuse Frank," Pearl was saying. "Things have been rather difficult for him lately."

His anger grew. *Defending Frank again!*

Then it hit him like a lead ball to the stomach. It wasn't anger at all. It was fear. He was scared stiff that Frank's behavior today and the drinking binges he'd been going on didn't have anything to do with Windom Institute or their parents' deaths. *What if Frank's behavior was his way of dealing with his frustrated love for Pearl?*

Memories flashed through his mind as though he were looking at them through a stereoscope. Frank arguing for the right to drive Pearl home from their farm; Frank leaping to defend her honor against Ed Ray's vile comments; Frank getting drunk for the first time the night of the dance—was it because Jason had pushed him aside to defend Pearl's honor himself? He claimed he wanted to attend Windom Institute but he stayed on the farm instead of finding a job that would pay his tuition. Was it to be nearer Pearl?

His large hand massaged baby Sara's back while the fear he'd been fighting for months burned inside him like acid. Were his wife and brother in love with each other?

sixteen

The children chatted excitedly beneath heavy lap robes in the back of the wagon, listing the places they wanted to stop on the Christmas shopping trip. Pearl hadn't seen so much anticipation and joy in their faces since their parents died. The day away from the farm would be good for them.

Good for Jason, too. He and his brothers had been butchering this week. All of them hated the job, hated taking the lives of the animals they'd cared for so faithfully, but no one mentioned it. It had to be done. Perhaps today would wipe some of the memory of it from their minds.

Sunlight glinted off the snow, making the already bright day brighter. The runners which had replaced the wheels for easier travel squeaked as they glided over the snow. Clouds rushed from the horses' mouths and frost coated the mufflers wrapped around the family members' faces.

The clear day offered a beautiful view of the river valley from the bluff which towered over the business section. Smoke from the store chimneys and the six stacks from the railroad roundhouse rose straight and tall in the crisp air. Jason and his large, shaggy, blanket-covered work team had all they could do to keep the wagon on its runners under control as they started down the steep street from the top of the bluff.

The town had changed radically during her lifetime, Pearl thought. Barely three hundred people lived in the town when she was born. Now there were almost two thousand. She'd been glad to read in the newspaper that tubular gas lights had been put in at the train station house last week. Her experience with the tramp back in August was one she didn't care to relive.

The millineries, pharmacies, clothing stores, hardware store, furniture store, jewelry stores, and general store all had their windows filled with Christmas displays, and nothing would do but they had to stop and admire each one. Maggie, Grace, and Pearl were captivated by the dolls and miniature furniture arranged in a Christmas party at Heiberg and Torgerson's, while the men preferred the carving of a Viking ship.

They stopped at Sherdahl's jewelry store—not to purchase but to allow the children to see his electric lights. Maggie and Andrew peered closely at them, fascinated, but Grace hid behind Jason's legs and wanted nothing to do with the strange bulbs that held no flame or odor. Andrew tried to hide his excitement and pride when Mr. Sherdahl invited him along with Jason and Frank to view the two horsepower engine that drove the lights and machinery in his store.

When they left, Jason spoke again of his desire to see the town establish an electrical service, listing its benefits as though the family hadn't already heard his arguments on the subject numerous times.

"You're a farmer now," Frank reminded him. "I'd think you'd be more interested in farmers rather than townspeople having electrical service."

That ended the conversation but sparked a strange thought for Pearl. It did seem Jason was born a city man. His conversations often centered on improvements for Chippewa City. He had dreams for the town, the same as Dr. Matt. It was Frank, although determined to continue his education, who went to the Grange meetings and read *The Progressive Farmer* until it was rags.

Jason and Frank had some business to attend to so they left the others for a bit. Jason promised to meet them at Dr. Matt's pharmacy in an hour.

The first stop for Pearl and the children was Bergh's General Store. Pearl wanted to find something for Jason before he returned.

Running a finger lightly over the top of a carved wooden collar box, she frowned and looked over a display: collar boxes, cuff boxes, work boxes, jewelry boxes. Jason wouldn't have much need of these now that he was on the farm instead of dressing daily as a rising young architect with a town office.

With Andrew's help, she decided on flannel slippers with lambswool liners. They would keep Jason's feet warm against the winter drafts that plagued their home in spite of the hay piled around the foundation. Besides, the gift was thoughtful without being personal. With their unusual relationship, she felt her options were limited.

Before leaving the store, Pearl and the girls admired the silk and woolen mufflers, the latest novelties in dress goods and trimmings, plush cloaks and jackets, and ladies' shawls. Andrew was more interested in warm winter boots, hats, and gents' duck coats.

When they made their way to Dr. Matt's pharmacy, a crowd of children was huddled around the show window. The Sterling children were as fascinated as the rest at the reproduction World's Fair Ferris wheel, its baskets in constant motion and loaded with dolls.

Bells chimed merrily as they entered. Jason entered right behind them. The warmth of the potbellied stove felt good to Pearl. Dr. Matt wasn't in, but Mr. Jenson, one of his clerks, greeted them cheerfully in his rolling Scandinavian accent.

"We want to look at dolls," Grace told Mr. Jenson importantly. Pearl and Jason exchanged delighted smiles over her head.

The clerk grinned from ear to ear. "You came to da right place, you betcha. Ve haf a t'ousand dolls; largest assortment ever brought to dis city." He looked at Jason. "Anyv'ere from one penny to two dollars. Everyt'ing in da store priced to suit da hard times, you betcha."

The toy department was a children's paradise. They passed

tin toys, iron toys, wood toys, musical toys, mechanical toys, toy beds and cradles, toy trunks, drums, rocking horses, shooflies, tea sets, toy furniture, banks, games of every description, hand sleds, storybooks, picture books, scrapbooks, panorama books; the variety seemed endless.

Grace was unaffected by it all, heading straight for the wall covered with dolls. After fifteen minutes of carefully listening to her critical review of numerous samples, Pearl and Jason left her alone with them and looked about the rest of the store.

They found Maggie admiring a display of autograph albums and scrapbooks, so popular with young girls and ladies. Andrew was lost in the book department among the dime novels. Pearl smiled at Jason and shook her head. Would Andy's desire for adventure ever wane?

When they returned to the toy department, Grace was cradling a doll in her arms. It was porcelain, about eight inches long, with soft brown hair and eyes that opened and closed. It was difficult to convince her to leave the doll behind.

When the children finally drifted off to other stores to complete their own Christmas purchases, Maggie taking Grace with her, Jason and Pearl were free to do their shopping.

Of course, the doll with the eyes that opened and closed was a must for Grace. It was their first purchase.

At Pearl's question, Jason explained that their money wasn't so tight they would have to be "stingy" with their giving. The children had all been patient in asking for things for the last few months while Jason learned the basics of the family finances and running the farm. He felt they could afford a piece of clothing at a reasonable price for each child, and the doll for Grace. With the small gifts the children would be exchanging among themselves, it should be sufficient.

When they passed the lot where the town hall and opera hall were to be built the following spring, Pearl noticed Jason's gaze linger over the sight and his lips tighten. She recalled happening upon him one evening in the parlor, sketching his idea of the future building. He'd flushed when he realized she'd recognized it and tossed the paper into the parlor stove, neither of them saying a word. She hurt for him but his willing sacrifice for his family only increased her love.

It was such fun shopping together, having friendly arguments over the most appropriate gifts, feeling Jason's hand at her elbow, shopkeepers nodding at them and calling them Mr. and Mrs. Sterling, as though they were one entity.

A stop at Kent's Confectionery and Bakery resulted in a few pieces of bright ribbon candy, oranges from California, and apples from New York to place in the Christmas stockings.

They chose a blouse of dainty French flannel for Maggie. Pearl was almost through making a school dress of the softest pale gray wool for Grace and she purchased black braid for trim to complete it.

It was difficult to choose for Andrew. When Pearl moved to the farm in August, he was two inches shorter than Maggie. Now he was just barely taller and no telling how much more he'd grow. None of his clothes hung right on him anymore. They finally settled on a pair of leather boots, which were costly at just over five dollars but which were sorely needed. Pearl would try cutting down some of Frank's old slacks and shirts for the boy after the holidays.

When she asked about Frank, all Jason would say was that he'd already purchased his gift. His reticence made her curious.

A pictorial album of Chippewa City in blue leather with gold print, just published by a local photographer, was chosen for Dr. Matt. A porcelain heart pin, adorned with tiny painted pansies surrounding the word "Mother" in gold script, caught Pearl's attention. During the last few months she'd grown to appreciate Boston's sacrifices for her and Johnny in new ways. Perhaps this pin. . . .

"Would you like it for Boston?" Jason asked.

She shifted her gaze to other pieces in the display case, not wanting him to see how badly she desired the piece. "We can find something else. The price is quite dear."

"We'll take it," he told the clerk.

She spun to face him and he smiled at her with a tenderness that tugged at her heart. "We'll take it," he repeated.

"Thank you." Her gaze tangled with his. It wasn't until the clerk handed them the small package wrapped in brown paper and tied with red twine that she realized with an embarrassed start they were still staring at each other with silly smiles. The memory of it made her incredibly self-conscious through the dinner at a local restaurant. She queried the others about their shopping throughout the meal, glad for a reason to avoid Jason's eyes. An excitement that had nothing to do with Christmas buzzed beneath the surface, making her giddy.

After dinner, they stopped to watch kids sledding down the bluff, which dropped sharply from the prairie to the old river bottom where Main Street was built. It offered the only challenging sledding for miles. When one of the boys offered to let Andrew use his coaster for a run, he grasped at the chance. "Can I, Jase? I'll take Grace along."

Jason rubbed his chin, watching the kids whizzing past. The town fathers didn't approve of sledding in this part of town, with the busy main street at the bottom of the hill filled with horses, delivery wagons, and buggies. Still, he was too close to boyhood himself not to remember the thrill of that bluff.

"All right. But don't forget what Dr. Matt said about all the loose teeth and broken bones he's seen from sledding the last few weeks."

It wasn't but a few minutes before Grace's laughing face zoomed past, Andy's arms shielding her from any possible harm. When the girl ran up to them, Pearl straightened her red crotched bonnet. "Was that fun?"

"Yes! We went fast! Faster than horses! And snow came up and splashed on my face!" She tossed mittened hands in the air to demonstrate, giggling until her sparkling eyes and red lips seemed to meet.

The new Shakespearean Ice Rink beside the mill was next. It was fun to be on ice skates again. Grace was new to the sport, and her eyes were huge as Pearl and Jason skated along with her between them. When she was finally brave enough to try it on her own, she was on her chin or her bottom as often as on her skates but those falls did nothing to dent her spirits.

If only people could keep that unconquerable zest throughout the true difficulties in life, Pearl thought, watching Grace once again struggle laughing to her feet. *Some people did, people like Jason.*

Her gaze drifted to Frank, who was gloomily watching Amy skate past with Ed Ray. Why was it that Frank took the easy road of complaint and excuses? Why did he refuse to hope and work for a better time?

Her thoughtful wanderings were cut short when Jason caught her hands as he darted past, pulling her about in a whirling circle and laughing down at her. "Skate with me, Mrs. Sterling," he implored, slowing to draw her against his side, taking one of her gloved hands in his own.

They skated perfectly together, a unison born of skating together many times in the past. His breath was a gentle warm rush against her cheek when he leaned closer to share a thought or a comment on one of the other skaters. It made her heart race and her legs threaten to weaken if he removed his arm.

"By Henry! Frank's actually loosened up and is skating with a girl. I don't believe it!"

She quickly found the couple in the crowd. Amy Henderson was smiling up at Frank's slender face, her hand tucked securely in his. Pearl's breath caught in a happy little gasp.

Jason went stiff beside her and pulled away a fraction. Pearl looked up at him in surprise. Chilly air sliced between them where before there had been only warmth. His brow furrowed into a scowl as he watched Frank and Amy.

Confused, she looked back at the couple. Another couple was skating nearby. Miranda and Grant. So that was the reason for the change in Jason! Hopelessness wiped away the joy that filled her only moments before. *Would Jason never get over loving Miranda?*

She lifted her chin and swallowed the tears that formed a large knot in her throat. Hadn't she been admiring Grace's pluck only an hour ago? Had she so soon forgotten love hopeth all things? They'd only been married a few months. God hadn't put a time limit on hope, saying one could give up hoping when it seemed difficult or unendurably long. She wouldn't let herself quit hoping for her husband's love!

Pearl leaned into Jason's side, ignoring the pain that flashed through her at the way he seemed to stiffen further at her action.

"Today has been wonderful."

The look he gave her held no joy.

She forced herself to continue smiling. "We'd best be getting home soon. We'll all be exhausted tomorrow if we stay much longer."

Without comment, he stopped near the bonfire where Andy was eating popcorn with a number of other skaters. Leaving her, he gathered up Maggie and Grace. Frank had decided to attend a soap bubble party and taffy pulling at the banker's residence—one of the community's attempts to follow Rev. Conrad's advice to draw the town's young people away from the saloons and billiard halls.

"How will he get home?" Pearl asked.

"He'll find a way," was Jason's curt reply.

Her heart sank. After the friendliness of the last few weeks, were they going to be drawn into another period of silent hostility?

Without physical activity to keep them warm, the winter cold penetrated their clothing and the robes covering them in the bobsled. Even the bricks that they'd warmed beside the bonfire before leaving didn't keep Pearl warm. But then, her heart was frozen.

Once at home, Andy stirred up the embers in the kitchen stove while Jason took care of the horses. Then everyone hurried about hiding their purchases from possible prying eyes. When the stove was hot enough, Pearl made hot chocolate and everyone gathered about the kitchen table.

She put bricks and irons on the stove to warm while they visited, as she did every night, to be wrapped in clean rags and used to warm the beds, as there was no heat in the bedrooms other than that which rose from the first story through small square registers in the bedroom floors.

Soon the household was in bed. After the stimulation of the day, Pearl couldn't sleep. She mixed buckwheat batter and set it on the back of the stove to rise for breakfast. Still restless, she took the school dress she was working on for Grace into the kitchen and stitched the braid in a fancy pattern along the hem and sleeves by the light of the kerosene lamp.

Two hours later she heard Jason's step on the stairs. He stood beside her chair awkwardly. "Couldn't sleep?"

She shook her head. Was he sorry, too, for the stiffness between them this evening?

He reached out to touch a sleeve of the dress, which looked especially delicate next to his large, callused hands. "It's pretty. I saw you teaching Grace to sew the other night."

"She's six; it's time she learned. She's trying to hemstitch a handkerchief and is determined to give it to Mother Boston for Christmas."

"You do a lot for my family." *His* family. The definition

hurt her.

His eyes searched hers and she wondered what he was trying to find there. She didn't realize she was holding her breath until she released it when he moved to a window.

"Worrying about Frank?" he asked.

She shook her head. "No. At least tonight there's no storm for him to get lost in. Actually, I'd forgotten he was still out."

"Forgotten?" His one word exploded with accusation. What had she done now?

He ran a hand through his already tousled hair in the gesture that had become so familiar to her. The despair in his face cut into her chest. "I don't remember when I've been as terrified as I was the night of the storm, wondering if he was lying dead out there. Hoped the experience would be enough to stop his drinking." He spread his hands helplessly. "What should I do for him? What would Dad have done? I just don't know what to do."

She looked down at her stitches. "We can only keep praying for him until God shows us something He wants us to say or do." *What else was there to do?* They were both too young and inexperienced with life to know the answers to things like this, she thought.

Jason dropped into a kitchen chair and rested his head in his hands, dejection in every line of his body. "Sometimes I think God must get downright weary of hearing me ask Him about Frank."

"Proverbs says 'Hope deferred maketh the heart sick: but when the desire cometh, it is a tree of life.' It's natural to become discouraged waiting for the things we hope for. That doesn't mean we'll never see what we desire. God will answer our prayers for Frank."

Jason propped his chin on the palm of his hand. "You've been studying scripture verses on hope for some time now. What is it you're hoping for so hard?"

A smile started on her lips and grew until she wondered whether it would ever stop. Could he read the answer in her eyes?

"I'll tell you when my hope is fulfilled."

🙢

The morning chores were completed, breakfast eaten, the dishes done, and the children off to school before Frank came home in the company of Sheriff Amundson the next day.

Jason and Pearl hurried out to meet the wagon as it pulled up at the gate, Pearl pulling a shawl about her shoulders on the way.

Frank's angry eyes challenged Jason's from beneath black brows when the sheriff said in his Norwegian accent, "Frank here has been fined five dollars. Didn't haf the money to pay, but I figgered you'd be good fer it, Yason."

"What's the charge?"

"He vas arrested vit a number of ot'er men last night—some of t'em prominent businessmen—in a raid on the gambling den over Plummer's Saloon."

tiny waist. Pearl's own checked gray flannel house dress seemed inordinately dowdy in comparison and she hoped fervently that Jason wouldn't return until the visitor left.

She hung Miranda's cloak on the pegs behind the kitchen door and indicated the rocking chair beside the stove. "Won't you sit down? If I'd expected you, I'd have started a fire in the parlor stove. I'll just put on some coffee for us."

"My, but you are the domestic little woman, aren't you?"

Her glance darted suspiciously at Miranda, who was gracefully adjusting her skirt. Had she imagined the sarcastic undertone?

Miranda looked up at her innocently and smiled. "What do you with your days out here?"

"The same thing most housewives do with their days: Care for the home and family."

"Does it seem terribly dreary after living in town? I seldom see you at the socials or dances."

Why, oh why had she come? Her very presence seemed to taint the atmosphere of their home. "Dreary?" She kept her voice light and smiled airily back at her guest. "Spending time with my new husband?"

Miranda's lips stiffened slightly. "Ah, but there are so many others underfoot." Her fingers moved to play with the delicate cameo pin at her neck.

The brooch Jason had given Miranda for Christmas only last year! Pain and fury twisted feverishly in Pearl's stomach. No true lady would flaunt such a gift in front of a man's wife.

Frank's taunt rang in her thoughts—*How easy will life be for you, living out your years with a man who loves another woman?* She slammed the door of her mind against the words, and brought to mind a picture of herself tucking into her hope chest the memory of Jason and herself praying together for his family.

It calmed her. "This is Jason's family's home. We do not consider his family an imposition and do not allow our guests to speak of them as such."

In spite of Miranda's assurance that she had stopped to call in order to repair their friendship—"it is the Christmas season, after all"—Pearl found the visit most uncomfortable and impatiently wished Miranda would leave.

"Have you and Mr. Tyler set your wedding date?"

"Not yet." Miranda dropped her gaze self-consciously to her lap. "Grant does pester me to agree to a date until his insistence is almost improper, but I feel it isn't wise for a woman to agree to marry so quickly. Don't you feel the same?"

"Yes, I do. Providing the couple doesn't know each other well."

Miranda's fingertips flew to her pursed lips. "Oh, my dear, I do apologize. I'd forgotten you and Jason married so impulsively."

Of course she hadn't forgotten! Pearl looked demurely down at the fine china cup in her lap. "When two people are very much in love. . . ." She shrugged daintily.

She had the satisfaction of noticing Miranda's lips tighten momentarily.

"I was disappointed not to receive an invitation to your wedding. But I forgive you, dear. Grant and I hope that you and Jason will attend our wedding, just the same."

Pearl set her cup and saucer on the table, avoiding an answer. If Miranda called her "dear" once more, she would scream!

"Since I wasn't at your wedding, won't you show me your wedding gown?"

"I don't think. . . ."

Miranda was already standing. "I do so love beautiful gowns. The master bedchamber is this way, is it not?"

Pearl hurried behind her, furious at Miranda's brazen manner.

Miranda didn't hesitate at the bedchamber door, but walked in as though it were her own.

She looks like she's cataloging every detail, Pearl thought angrily as Miranda's eyes darted about the room.

The unwelcome guest stopped beside the dressing table and ran the tip of her index finger along Pearl's mother-of-pearl hand-mirror. "All your lovely toiletries. Does your husband have none of his own?"

Their eyes met in the mirror, Pearl refusing to look away from Miranda's amused gaze.

"The gown must be in here." Miranda pulled open the doors of the handsome cherry clothespress, and ran her hand along the gowns hanging there. "Why, this holds only your clothing." She turned to face Pearl, a self-satisfied smile spreading across her round face. "Jason isn't sharing your bedchamber, is he?"

eighteen

"I believe it's time you left, Miss Sibley."

Pearl almost went limp in relief and gratitude at the sound of Frank's voice, rigid with constrained fury. When had he come up behind them?

He strode across the room and grabbed Miranda by the arm. "Allow me to escort you out."

"Frank, let go of me this instant!" She jerked her arm but he only tightened his grasp on the voluminous Nile-green sleeve and hurried her toward the stairway. "You're hurting me!"

Pearl hurried along behind them telling herself she should insist Frank unhand their guest, but she couldn't get the words out.

Frank grabbed Miranda's lovely cloak from the peg and threw it into her arms. Yanking open the door, he shoved her through it. "Don't ever come to this house again."

The door slammed between them, closing off Miranda's indignant face.

"I don't know how to thank you. I couldn't think how to stop her, and. . . and. . . how could anyone be so dreadful?" To her horror, tears shook her last words.

Frank propped his fists against his hips. "Why didn't you tell that imitation of a lady to leave yourself?"

She wiped her fingers across her cheeks to catch any stray tears. "I'm surprised at you. A lady would never do such a thing."

His guffaw brought a trembling smile to her lips and she hiccuped. "Jason mustn't know what she said."

"He won't hear it from me," he promised. "My big brother should thank God daily that he's not in that woman's clutches. Imagine spending your life with something like that!"

"She isn't all bad," Pearl defended automatically.

"Well, he got a much better deal with you. He's a good man. He deserves a good wife."

"You're no longer angry with him?" Surprise tinged her question.

He shrugged. "Not his fault Mom and Dad died or that the country is so strapped financially." He ducked his head self-consciously. "I just wish he'd quit treating me like a kid or a hired hand. I'm only a couple years younger than he is and I was raised on the farm, too. Do you think he ever asks my opinion about how anything should be handled around here? He does not! Why he even talks things over with you and you're just a woman!" He flushed. "I'm sorry, I didn't mean. . . ."

"I understand." Another time she would have argued that women have as much intelligence as men but she didn't want to stop his confidence. It's true Jason discussed the business of the farm with her often. His sharing meant a great deal to her. She knew how uncommon it was for a man to discuss business with a woman.

"I just wish he'd treat me like an equal," Frank was saying.

She linked her fingers loosely in front of her. "I don't believe Jason realizes the way you feel. Taking on the burden of the farm and the family is the only tangible way Jason knows to deal with the grief of losing your parents. It's the last thing he can give them—the only thing he can give them now."

Frank's deep brown eyes met hers. "How does he expect me to deal with my grief?"

She had no answer.

He leaned back until the chair stood on only two legs. "I've been doing a lot of thinking. Figured Jason would be ready to wallop me when the sheriff brought me home, but the only thing I saw in his face was disappointment." He shook his head slowly. "Hurt me a lot more than anything he could say or do."

A flush spread up his neck and the chair dropped back to all four legs. "What you said about being a man Amy could love—well, I've been considering that. You're right. With every passing week I've become more like men I don't respect—men like Ed Ray. Amy deserves a man of strong character, like Jason."

Thank You, Lord! her heart cried. "Jason isn't perfect," she said cautiously. "He makes mistakes like everyone else. I believe the strength he does have comes from leaning on Christ's strength."

Frank propped his elbows on his knees and examined his fingertips as though they held the secret of life. "Along with being angry with Jason, I've been pretty mad at God, too. Couldn't stop thinking about the things you said a few weeks back about God meeting us where we are and forgiving us— though believe me, I tried to forget! This afternoon, I told Him I was sorry. I mean to follow Him from now on, with His help."

Knowing an emotional display would only embarrass him, she refrained from grasping his hands as she wanted to do and settled for a simple, "I'm glad." One hope that had become a tree of life!

"I realized it wasn't Jason or God that was messing up my life. I'm doing a pretty bang-up job of it all by myself. If I was attending Windom Institute right now, I would have been suspended after last night. Using intoxicating drinks and frequenting saloons and billiard halls is cause for expulsion."

"Yes, I know."

"Heard Amy with my own ears saying she wouldn't court

any young men who drink and even that didn't stop me. Figured I hadn't a chance with her anyway, so what did it matter? After she hears I've added gambling to my vices. . . ."

"Shouldn't that be past tense?"

He snorted. "It's definitely past tense. Only good thing about last night is that Ed Ray was hauled in by the sheriff, too. At least Amy will know the truth about him now."

He sucked in his lips beneath his thin black mustache and took a deep breath. "Do you think I have any chance with Amy, after all the dumb things I've done?"

"Only she can answer that."

The chair almost fell over when he stood up. His hands slid nervously down his jean-covered thighs and back up again. "Think I'll ride into town tonight. I'd kind of like to tell her about last night myself before she hears it from someone else. Maybe then she'll believe me when I tell her I'm turning over a new leaf."

This time she gave in to her impulse and gave him a quick hug. "Welcome back, Frank."

"Welcome back to what?" Jason's words were colder than the winter air that whistled through the open door behind him.

nineteen

"Oh, no!" Pearl yanked the oven door open with a hand loosely wrapped in her voluminous apron. Waving away the smoke, she grabbed the cookie sheet and dropped it on top of the stove. Every cookie was as black as coal.

Almost as black as Jason's eyes when he'd found her standing with her hands on Frank's shoulders yesterday afternoon. For a moment she'd thought he was jealous. Ridiculous thought! More likely, his militant expression was the result of meeting Miranda on his way back from town. There wasn't any way they could have missed passing each other.

Joy and relief had routed the anger from his eyes when Frank told him he'd decided to mend his ways and had committed his life to Christ. Still, his gaze held some doubt after Frank left the room. Didn't he think Frank would stick by his decision?

How had Amy responded to his news last evening, she wondered, dropping teaspoonfuls of gingersnap dough on a greased pan. She wasn't about to broach such a potentially delicate subject, despite her curiosity.

As though on cue, Frank came inside. Yanking off his boots, he dropped his work gloves on the table and came over to hold his hands out to the stove's warmth. He cleared his throat and said as though in answer to her thoughts, "Saw Amy last night."

"Oh?"

"She was incredible."

Pearl's throat contracted at the awe in his voice. If only Jason cared for her so much!

"I wasn't certain she'd even allow me the chance to speak, with the rumors about my drinking going around. But she invited me into their parlor, and I told her all the stupid things I've done the last few months—didn't dare leave anything out. Figured I'd rather she heard it from me than from someone else.

"Then I told her about my decision to live the way I thought Christ would want. She seemed pretty glad about that, so I packed up my courage and told her I'd like to court her. Could have knocked me off that dainty little parlor chair with a feather when she agreed to it."

"I'm so glad for you, Frank!"

He gave her an embarrassed smile. "It seems her father has other ideas. Said no way a man with my rotten reputation was going to be seen with his daughter. I tried to explain that I've changed my ways but he wouldn't believe it."

"I'm sorry."

"Finally he said he'll reconsider. . . ."

"Frank!"

He grimaced. "In a year. If I stay sober and out of trouble for a year, he'll reconsider allowing me to see Amy—if Amy is still willing."

Poor boy! It had taken a lot of courage to make the decision to turn his life around and to tell Amy everything before he even knew whether she cared for him. The disappointment must seem devastating.

"A year sounds like a long time, but at least there's hope."

"I don't understand. God has forgiven me. Why can't Amy's father?" His eyes searched her face for an answer.

She slid her hands into her apron pockets. "God can see your heart but Amy's father can only judge you by your actions."

A long minute passed while he stared gloomily at the stove. "I hate to admit it, but you're right."

Would he take offense at her next question? It came out haltingly. "You. . . you didn't decide to become a Christian only to please Amy, did you?"

His gaze met hers steadily, and a smile warmed his eyes. "No. That decision stands, no matter what else happens."

⁊ა

The week before Christmas went by in a whirl of activities that put a sparkle of anticipation in everyone's eyes. Maggie and Andrew reluctantly fit studying for an algebra examination into their already full days of classes, studying, and chores. There were no complaints, however, when asked to help with the baking, candy making, or corn popping!

Grace's favorite holiday preparation was making cornucopias. The pride in her smile when she completed her first paper cone, complete with ribbon for hanging and trim of braid from a dress Pearl had made, was a memory Pearl was sure would live in her heart for the rest of her life. No one mentioned that the cornucopia was slightly lopsided or that any small items would be in danger of slipping out the bottom.

The six-year-old's help increased the time it took to do the Christmas baking, but neither Pearl or Maggie minded in the least, as Grace's obvious enjoyment added to their own Christmas joy.

One evening Jason brought out a round wooden box and carefully removed three roughly carved wooden figures—Joseph, Mary, and the baby Jesus. When Pearl exclaimed over them, Jason said, "Dad carved these when I was no older than Grace. He said many times a house should have a reminder of what we're celebrating at Christmas."

The figures were placed on the round, marble-topped table in the middle of the parlor. Grace often abandoned her dolls to play with the wooden family over the next few days and never tired of listening to the Christmas story—or repeating it, though her interpretations varied slightly each time!

Friday, December 22, kept the entire family busy with the last-minute holiday cleaning, including polishing the nickel and cleaning the isinglass window on the fancy parlor stove, strewing tea leaves over the parlor carpet and brushing it well, trimming wicks and washing lamp chimneys.

As soon as the supper dishes were done, Jason brought in the barrels of greens from New York which he'd purchased in town, along with fine wire and twine. In a gesture that had warmed Pearl's heart, he'd purchased a barrel for the poor farm, also.

The greens were piled on top of the table, spilling the delightful pine fragrance into the air. The family gathered around to form the branches into garlands and wreaths. They chatted eagerly while they worked, teasing each other about the gifts Santa Claus would bring, the children sharing recitations from the Christmas program presented at school that day.

Jason looked across the spicy, forest-green pile, and his fingers stopped wrapping the wire with which he'd been working. Pearl's face was filled with a sweet contentment that constricted his heart. If only he could believe she was truly happy here in his home!

The day they'd gone Christmas shopping, his heart had almost burst with happiness at being with her, at her sweet, unusually shy smile, at the way she'd fit so naturally into his arms when they'd skated. Then he'd pointed out Frank and Amy, and Pearl's gasp reminded him that he didn't hold his wife's heart.

After Grace had been tucked in bed, the rest of the family gathered to decorate the parlor. They wouldn't have a Christmas tree but they had the greens to put up. They all wanted the sight of the decorated room to be a surprise for Grace.

Under Maggie and Pearl's direction, the men hung the

garlands, swagging them from the hanging lamp to the corners of the room, attaching them to the picture rail next to the
ceiling. More garlands were roped like trim along the fringed
edges of the velvet draperies. The pictures on the wall didn't
escape. Greenery was hung over the tops of the frames and
wound around the wires attaching the pictures to the picture
rail.

Jason and Andrew were assigned the task of hanging the
roping over the doorway between the dining room and parlor.
Frank and Pearl were laughing as they trimmed the railing of
the staircase. The sound cut Jason to the quick and made him
strangely tired.

Had he ever felt as young and carefree as the two of them
seemed tonight, laughing and teasing together? He felt ninety
years old, with the weight of six lives and a farm on his shoulders.

Did Pearl feel that way, too? What a gift to her this marriage has been, he thought bitterly. He'd loaded her young
life with responsibilities and done precious little to relieve
her load. Perhaps that was what Frank gave her—laughter
and youth and freedom and dreams. She needed that; everyone did.

Pearl had given that to him. His hands froze on the prickly
pine. It was true. By becoming his wife and helping him
carry his load, she'd given him the freedom to be true to himself and his values. The desire to win her love had given him
a dream to replace Miranda and the career he'd given up.

He stepped off the stool. Picking up some of the remaining
greens, he moved into the dining room, urging Andrew to join
him. There wasn't enough garland left to trim that room as
elaborately as the parlor, but they could place the greens about
the picture frames and on top of the china closet and door-
ways.

Escaping the room didn't allow him the luxury of escaping

his thoughts. He'd been unfair to Pearl, marrying her as he did. Not that he didn't love her. But he knew better than to think love justified such a selfish action as marrying someone who didn't return his love.

He should have been honest with her, admitted his love for her. Instead he'd tried to manipulate her heart and her life as surely as Miranda had tried to manipulate his with her announcement that she wouldn't marry him unless he let his family fend for themselves.

Miranda. At the thought of her he jerked the garland apart more savagely than he'd intended. What had she meant to accomplish, coming out to the farmstead the other day? She'd been turning from the farm lane onto the road when he met her as he returned from town. The sight of her had sent a combination of fear and fury rushing through his veins and he'd passed her by with only a nod.

When the others retreated to the kitchen, he remained behind to bank the fire in the parlor stove and put out the lamps. One had to be especially careful of fire hazards with greens in the house.

Frank was in his boots and buttoning his coat when Jason entered the kitchen. His younger brother grinned at him with a friendliness that gripped his heart. It was good to have the bitterness gone from Frank's face and voice. "I'm going to run out and check on the animals one last time before turning in."

Jason watched him from between the blue curtains of the kitchen window, hands in his pockets. Pearl joined him and his heart pumped faster. When he glanced down, her eyes were shining up at him. "It's wonderful to see him so happy, isn't it?"

He couldn't get his throat to work, so he only nodded. Did she love Frank so much that his happiness could bring such joy to her face? Had he destroyed all chance of happiness for himself—and Pearl and Frank, too—by tying Pearl to him with their "friendly" marriage?

He should have the courage to ask whether she and Frank loved each other, but he didn't. Something inside him would shrivel up and die if she admitted to loving Frank.

He forced his gaze away from her. "At least some apparent good has come from the raid Frank was arrested in last week—in addition to his commitment to Christ. Did you see the new town ordinance in the paper?"

Her hair brushed his arm as she shook her head, sending shivers along his nerves. "No."

"The ordinance prohibits saloons and other public places from having pool tables, billiard tables, pigeonhole tables, or cards, dice, musical instruments, or other entertainment where liquor is sold. No chairs, tables, stands, counters, or seats will be allowed in establishments that sell liquor—only a bar and seats for employees behind the bar."

She slipped her hand beneath his arm and squeezed it excitedly and he stuffed his hands deeper into his pockets to avoid drawing her into his arms. "That's wonderful! At least young men won't be so blatantly tempted to gamble any longer. God can make good come out of anything, can't He?"

A small smile tugged at the edges of his mouth. "Yes, out of anything." Even out of the marriage he'd botched?

The wish to have her with him like this always, the joy in her eyes due to her love for him instead of Frank, was like a physical pain. She was fine and wonderful; he'd never believe anything less of her. If she did love Frank, she'd never act on that love and be unfaithful. Frank wouldn't be dishonorable either, not in that way, despite the drinking and gambling he'd fallen into—especially now that he'd decided to change.

But he wanted more than Pearl's faithfulness; he wanted her love.

His gaze slipped to the sampler on the wall above Pearl's head. "Charity hopeth all things." How many times had he heard or read that over the years? He hadn't known living the verse would be so painful. In his youth, he'd been foolish enough to believe that loving made all things easy. It only made them possible.

When he'd asked Pearl to marry him, she'd said she wasn't in love with anyone. If she'd grown to love Frank, it was because Jason had brought her to his home.

He'd believed God would cause Pearl to love him. But could God work in a situation that was a result of selfishness such as his?

He can if one asks forgiveness. The thought was like a bright light in the darkness that had filled his heart. Had his failure to ask forgiveness for his selfish actions stood in God's way of answering his prayers and fulfilling his hope?

Jason's prayer was simple and direct, and left him feeling relieved. He didn't know what if any changes would result from his prayer but at least his unforgiveness would no longer stand in God's path as He worked in all of their lives.

૨ð

Early afternoon sunshine poured through the kitchen window Christmas Eve day to play on the packages and bright coffee tins filled with baked goods piled high on the table. Everyone but Jason was dressed and ready to leave.

Pearl grabbed a buttery sugar cookie from Grace's hand. "Be careful not to get anything on your pretty dress. You don't want it dirtied before Mother Boston and Dr. Matt see it, do you? It's so pretty!"

Grace grasped the edge of the table, shoulder high on her, with both hands and grinned up at her, the sparkle in her eyes showing plainly that she, too, thought her new dress was lovely.

It was. The ruby-red silk accentuated the excited flush of

her cheeks. The Mother Hubbard styling with the highstanding ruffled neck and puffed sleeves made her look deceptively angelic.

Pearl had thought she'd never get the child dressed and ready. Frank had taken her with him to hang suet on tree branches and sheaves of grain on fence posts for the birds and wild animals. It was a Christmas custom he'd learned from their Norwegian neighbors, Thor and Ellie, when he was just a child. Trust Frank with his love of animals to embrace the custom, Pearl thought.

The door opened, allowing Frank and crisp winter air to enter together. "Horses are harnessed." He indicated the items on the table with a slight wave of his gloved hand. "These ready to put in the bobsled?"

Pearl raised her hands to her cheeks and shook her head. "I hope so. What if I've forgotten something?"

"No harm done. Your family will be here tomorrow for dinner, anyway," he reassured her.

"I do wish you could be with us for dinner at my parents' tonight, Frank."

"Someone has to see to it the cows are milked this evening. But I'll try to meet you for church services afterward."

"Good." She turned about, only to find herself face to face with Jason, who had just entered the room, freshly shaved and dressed in his best gray suit, a high, round linen collar at his throat.

"My, you look handsome!"

A pleased look followed surprise across Jason's face. She wanted to melt right through the floor. Surely she hadn't said that! The snickers in the background assured her she had.

She watched his gaze swiftly take in her own turquoise silk with the dainty ribbon bow at the throat topping the jabot of cream-colored lace, and the wide ribbon accentuating her slender waist with a large bow in front.

"You're beautiful, Pearl."

The huskiness in his voice sent shivers skittering along her nerves.

"Aren't you two going to follow tradition?"

Perplexed, Pearl turned toward Maggie. "Follow. . .?"

Looking wide-eyed and innocent, Maggie pointed above Pearl's head.

Her heart sank to her stomach and beyond when she glanced up. Andrew had wired a kissing ball with mistletoe onto the end of a broom and was standing behind Jason, holding the abominable thing over their heads.

A quick glance at Jason showed he was as flustered as she. Andrew, Maggie, and Grace were wearing grins as wide as the Minnesota prairie.

"C'mon Jase, kiss her!" Andrew taunted.

Jason would never kiss her without her consent, she was certain. Still, her glance darted about the room, anywhere but Jason's face. Frank was leaning against the door, arms crossed over his chest, amusement in his eyes. The memory of his ridicule of Jason for not sharing her bedchamber flashed through her mind. She couldn't allow Jason to be embarrassed like that again.

She laid a hand on Jason's woolen sleeve. The smile she gave him when she lifted her face to meet his gaze was a triumph of courage over sheer terror.

"Merry Christmas, Jason."

For a moment she was afraid he would reject her offer. Then the surprise in his eyes turned to wonder and his hands gently cradled her waist.

"Merry Christmas, my love." The words were for her ears only. His gaze didn't leave hers as he bent to touch her lips with his.

Her eyelids drifted shut. His kiss was a thousand times sweeter than any of her dreams.

twenty

The children's hoots and applause slowly filtered through Jason's consciousness. Reluctantly he released Pearl's sweet lips. He tried to read her reaction in her eyes but she shielded her gaze from his with her lashes and moved swiftly to retrieve her cape from one of the kitchen chairs, avoiding looking at anyone.

Had his kiss embarrassed her frightfully? He recalled how she'd always hated parlor game kisses, believing kisses should be reserved for those one dearly loved and given reverently. He moved behind her and took her cape, helping her into it. She stiffened when he rested his hands on her shoulders. The delicate scent of lavender surrounded him and the soft touch of her hair against his cheek was like a taste of heaven as he whispered in her ear, "Thank you for not embarrassing me in front of my family."

He'd hoped she'd turn around into his arms. Instead she merely nodded and moved through the door.

Was it only to save his pride that she'd kissed him? For she had returned his kiss, he thought, following her to the bobsled, returned it warmly and sweetly.

At the sight of Frank helping her into the conveyance, his jaw all but locked. He forced it to relax as he moved around the back of the vehicle and climbed up himself. He even managed to smile as he waved good-bye to his brother.

The feel of Pearl's lips against his own was still with him. The sweet, willing manner in which she'd leaned against him and offered her kiss rekindled the hope and determination he'd allowed fear to almost extinguish. Pearl was his wife. He was going to do everything in his power to win her love. If

Frank loved her—well, that would have to be between Frank and God. Surely God meant another woman for Frank. It couldn't be God's will that he love his brother's wife.

He'd tell Pearl that evening, get his love out in the open, and trust the Lord to help them through whatever the future held.

Pearl had eagerly looked forward to spending Christmas Eve dinner with her stepparents and Johnny's family. Boston and Dr. Matt's home was decorated in greens, and large, floppy red bows accentuating the forest color. Fresh red carnations in the middle of the linen-covered dining room table added fragrant cheer.

Bayberry from the tapers lighting the table blended with the scents of pine and carnations, only to be lost with them to the smell of oyster soup, and later, succulent roast beef and gravy. Boston's best china, silver, and crystal reflected back the flickering light.

Anticipation of the church service and gift exchanging to come made everyone talkative during the meal. Yet Pearl had difficulty keeping her mind from straying to Jason's kisses. Once she even found her fingertips resting against her lips. Mortified, she removed them immediately, wondering whether Jason, seated beside her, had noticed and realized her thoughts.

Had she only imagined that he seemed especially solicitous and kind this evening? And the way he'd looked into her eyes and smiled—deliberately and warmly—as though she was the most special person in his world. At one point she'd had to catch herself from whispering "I love you."

That was when she became truly nervous. He'd asked for her to be his wife and housekeeper; he'd not asked for her love. It would only make things more uncomfortable for them both if she confessed her feelings for him.

But what of the words he'd whispered against her lips, her heart argued? What of those impossibly sweet whispered words—*Merry Christmas, my love*? They hovered in her thoughts like a promise throughout the evening.

She understood now what Boston had tried to tell her on her wedding day—understood that sacrificing and hoping and believing for one who doesn't return your love meant living with constant pain.

She was tired of hurting inside, tired of the continual longing for his love. Still, given the chance to marry him again, knowing what she knew now, her answer would be the same.

The families had agreed to exchange gifts among themselves before the service; Jason's family would exchange their own gifts in the morning.

Watching Grace's delight in her gifts gave Pearl a welcome reprieve from the emotions that had held her captive since Andrew appeared with the kissing ball. Johnny and Jewell gave Grace a lovely apron of India lawn with lace edging the square neckline, and nothing would do but that she try it on immediately over her red silk Christmas dress.

Boston and Dr. Matt's gift to Grace surprised everyone. It was the reproduction of the World's Fair Ferris wheel Dr. Matt had displayed in his pharmacy window, along with a tiny doll that fit in the wheel's baskets. Grace laughed and squealed, clapped and jumped up and down, unable to contain her excitement. Jason, Johnny, Billy, and Andrew were as taken with it as the little girl, and spent half-an-hour on the floor with the toy and Grace.

Pearl's most precious memory of the evening would be when Boston first saw the heart pin. From the tears that filled her eyes, Pearl knew she understood that from now on, she would always be Mother to her, and not Mother Boston. The love that had grown in her heart for Jason's brothers and sisters over the last few months had taught her how special Boston's devotion had been to her and Johnny.

True to his word, Frank joined them for church. Pearl knew it would be especially meaningful to him this year.

She loved hearing Rev. Conrad read the Christmas story in his rumbling deep voice. The Christmas service was always one of her favorites, the hope for the world becoming reality in the person of the baby Jesus.

Christ—the promised Messiah and Savior. Another hope that took a long time for fulfillment. She thought of the thousands of years that passed from the time of the promise to Christ's birth. Had people grown weary watching for the hope of a Savior to arrive?

Grace tugged on the leghorn sleeve of Pearl's turquoise dress and whispered loudly, "I know that story."

Pearl nodded, holding a finger to her lips. Grace faced forward again, sliding to the edge of the wooden pew, silently mouthing the words along with Rev. Conrad. Over her head, Jason and Pearl shared a smile that wrapped Pearl in a warm feeling of family and belonging.

After the services, the family scattered about the chapel, each seeking out special friends for a Christmas greeting. Maggie took Grace along with her, allowing Pearl to slip out to the wagon for the tins of cookies to exchange with friends.

The church was almost empty when she had distributed her gifts, and received *julekage*—a Swedish Christmas bread—and delicate golden rolls of lacy Scandinavian cookies called *krumkake* in return from Swedish friends. She hurried down the aisle to where Frank was speaking with Amy and her father.

"I don't blame you for not wanting me to court your daughter, Mr. Henderson," she heard Frank say. "I'd feel the same if I were her father. But. . . ."

She'd intended to ask Frank if he'd seen Jason, but realizing the seriousness of his conversation, she slipped past without being noticed by the three. A quick prayer rose from her heart for Frank as she entered the narthex.

Hearing Jason's voice coming from the cloak room, she started toward it. Her feet and heart came to an abrupt halt at Miranda's honeyed voice.

"Jason, I made an awful mistake when I called off our engagement. I only agreed to marry him to make you jealous. It's you I love, not Grant. If you have your marriage to Pearl annulled, I will still marry you."

twenty-one

The three miles home were the longest miles of Pearl's life. She tried valiantly to act as though she hadn't heard Miranda's offer to Jason, and smiled and laughed with the rest of the family. If her laughter seemed strained and pitched higher than usual, no one mentioned it. The jingling bells Frank had tied to the horses' harnesses and the Christmas hymns the family sang couldn't chase away her pain.

What had Jason answered Miranda? She hadn't stayed around to find out. She knew Jason's beliefs would never allow him to dissolve their marriage but those beliefs didn't prevent him from loving Miranda.

When he'd joined the rest of the family at the bobsled his jaw was set so firmly it could have been chiseled in ice. Was he thinking that he could have married Miranda if he hadn't been so hasty in asking Pearl to be his wife?

She didn't wait to be helped from the bobsled when they arrived home but climbed down herself and hurried inside, lighting the lamp with the bit of red flannel in it that sat on the kitchen table. A moment later she was stirring up the fire in the kitchen stove and announcing to those coming in behind her that she would be heating apple cider to warm them before they retired.

While Frank and Andy unharnessed the horses, Maggie and Grace warmed themselves beside the stove. Their cheeks and noses were red from the cold and wind, and their eyes sparkled with holiday joy.

Pearl entered the pantry to retrieve the cider and almost jumped when Jason's hands cupped her shoulders from behind. He took her cloak and whispered, "I'm going to start a fire in the parlor stove. Don't forget we have the stockings to fill after the others are in bed." He carried the cider jug to the kitchen for her.

Her hands were unsteady as she carried the cups to the table. Tonight of all nights she did not want to be alone with him! How could she possibly keep to herself the knowledge of the conversation she'd overheard? She needed time alone to pray and compose herself.

She warmed the *julekage* while the cider heated. The cardamom from the frosted bread and cinnamon sticks added a festive scent to the air as the group enjoyed the warmth of the apple cider.

"Hardly seems like Christmas without Mom and Dad." Andy's eyes glinted suspiciously.

The mood in the room changed drastically at his words.

"We all feel that way," Jason admitted.

There was a sheen in his eyes, too, and it shamed Pearl. She'd been so concerned with her own desire for Jason's love that she'd forgotten this was the family's first Christmas without their parents.

"Before we go off to bed," Jason was saying, "maybe we should all share our favorite Christmas memories of Mom and Dad. Kind of like Grace's scrapbook stories with a Christmas theme."

By the time everyone had shared a memory, tears brightened every eye and smiles touched every face.

"Dear Lord, our Father, thank Thee for making each of us a member of this family." Everyone's heads bowed as Jason began the unexpected prayer. "Thank Thee for giving us parents who loved us and Thee, and for the years Thou lent them to us, and for the wonderful memories they've left us. We thank Thee, also, for bringing Pearl into our lives and making us one family. In Jesus name, Amen."

Tears misted her eyes at Jason's inclusion of her in his prayer. Grace drove away the somber mood with an eager question. "Do we get to open more pwesents now?"

Maggie shook her head. "Not until tomorrow morning."

"Why?"

"You have to go to bed so Santa Claus can bring your presents. He can't come when you might see him, you know," Maggie explained patiently.

"He could have come when we were at church. We couldn't see him then."

Pearl grinned at the child's nimble reasoning.

Jason shook his head. "I was just in the parlor and there are no presents. Of course, it might be because there aren't any stockings hung up yet."

Grace gasped, her eyes huge. "My stocking!"

Maggie and Grace retrieved stockings for everyone. Maggie held her long ribbed wool stocking up. "At last this ugly, itchy, baggy thing will serve a purpose other than humiliating me."

Pearl smiled in sympathy from her own experiences with the uncomfortable necessity.

Grace frowned as the stockings were passed out to the appropriate family members. "Mine is the smallest." Her bottom lip jutted out and she sat down in the rocker, throwing herself in a slump against the back.

Jason picked up her stocking and held it alongside his, pursing his lips and pretending to study them seriously. "Guess mine is the biggest stocking here. How about if we trade? I didn't ask Santa for anything very big anyway."

Her pout rolled away and she threw out her arms in a silent offer of a hug. Jason complied, lifting her into his arms. "Thank you, Jason!"

He kissed her cheek. "You're welcome." His brows met. "Who do you think is more important, pumpkin—Jesus or Santa?"

Grace's face scrunched in serious concentration. "Jesus." Her head bounced in a decided nod.

"Why?"

"Well, Santa comes only at Chwistmas to bwing pwesents if we've been good. Jesus came at Chwistmas, too. But the pastor says Jesus stays with us all the time, in our hea'ts, and loves us even if we fo'get to be good."

Jason smiled. "That's exactly right."

Frank dug his hands into the pockets of his wool trousers. "Best sermon I've heard in a long time."

Jason grinned at him over Grace's head. "Now how about if you go up to bed with Maggie, pumpkin? Sooner you're asleep, the sooner Santa will come."

"Will you and Pearl come listen to my pwayers when I'm in bed?"

"Don't we always?"

She nodded vigorously. "But this is Chwistmas and I was afwaid you might fo'get."

He gave her an extra squeeze before setting her down. "We never forget you, pumpkin."

"Never," Pearl repeated, smiling at the little girl.

By the time they'd listened to Grace's prayers, Maggie and Andrew were ready to retire, also, and Pearl was dreading that the time alone with Jason was drawing near. She felt reprieved when they returned to the kitchen to find Frank still there.

She panicked immediately when Frank stood, raised his arms high over his head in a stretch, and said he was ready to turn in, too.

"I saw you speaking with Amy this evening," she said, hoping to delay him. "Did you give her a Christmas gift?"

Jason's head jerked toward her so swiftly she couldn't keep her gaze from meeting his. The shock in his eyes sent despair tumbling through her. How could she have been so thoughtless of Frank's confidence?

"I'm sorry, Frank. I forgot you hadn't told Jason."

Frank shrugged, and the startled look in his own eyes slipped away. "It's all right. No reason he shouldn't know, I guess."

Jason's brows met above troubled eyes. "Know what?"

He sounded as though he wasn't at all certain he wanted to hear the answer, Pearl thought.

Frank gripped the back of the kitchen chair in front of him. With a rather sheepish look he said, "About Amy Henderson. I. . . kind of like her. A lot."

Jason looked thunderstruck. He stared at his brother, his jaw hanging open. "You mean you. . . and Amy?"

Frank grimaced. "Well, there isn't any me and Amy yet." Succinctly, Frank told him the story.

Before he was done, Jason had lowered himself into one of the chairs and Pearl thought curiously that it looked for all the world as though his knees trembled in the process.

"Anyway, after church tonight, her father allowed me to speak with her." Frank took a deep breath, his grip on the chair tightening. "I told her I intended to follow through on my commitment not to drink or gamble but it was going to be mighty hard waiting a year to court her."

"What did she say?" Pearl asked.

"She said, 'Mr. Sterling, I'd be pleased to have you escort me to next year's Christmas Eve service. We can then thank the Lord together for giving you the strength to keep that commitment.'"

Frank's almost black eyes lifted to Pearl's. "It's like you told me. God meets us where we are. I wish I'd never tried the drinking and gambling route. Deep inside I knew it wouldn't help anything but I tried it anyway. Now I have to live with the consequences, including a year of not courting Amy." His grin was strained. "Guess if Jacob worked fourteen years for Rachel, I can make it through a year. With the Lord to lean on and with Amy's faith in me, there's no way

I'm going to backslide."

Pearl envied Amy such a love! It took her two attempts to speak. "You can trust Amy not to promise herself to another before you court her. She'll be waiting for you next Christmas and will give you the chance to win her heart forever."

Frank's eyes were hungry with the desire to believe her.

The legs of Jason's chair squeaked across the linoleum as he pushed it back and stood. He clapped a hand on his brother's shoulder. "Amy Henderson is a good woman. I hope you win her."

Pearl thought Frank's grin endearingly self-conscious.

"Why didn't you tell me about her before?" Jason demanded, giving his brother a friendly shake.

Frank brushed his hair off his forehead. "Guess I didn't want anyone feeling sorry for me or laughing at me if she wasn't interested."

"I'd be the last one to laugh at that."

Was he thinking of Miranda? Pearl wondered at his husky admission.

Jason pulled an envelope from an inner suit pocket. "Your gift from Pearl and me."

Questions filled Frank's eyes when he lifted them from the opened paper moments later. "A receipt for the winter term at Windom Institute."

Jason jammed his hands into his wool trouser pockets and nodded briskly. "I figure I can handle most of the work around here during the next few months, with you and Andrew helping out weekends and after school. We can re-evaluate in the spring, but we'll try to keep you in school as long as you want."

Frank reached out a hand and Jason gripped it. "Thanks, big brother. Way I see it, with the way the railroads and other businessmen keep taking chunks of profit from grain and livestock the farmers raise, a farmer's got to have a good education today in order to stand a fighting chance. Then too, there's the changing agricultural methods and farm machinery. Farmers 've got to keep up."

Jason's brow furrowed. "Reckon your right."

"When I get out of school, I'm going to do my share by this family so you can get back to being an architect." He looked down at the slip of paper in his hands and took a deep breath. "I've been trying to get up the courage to tell you. If things work out the way I hope, I'd like to run this farm one day."

She saw Jason swallow and she had to restrain herself from hugging her brother-in-law. This was Frank's true Christmas gift to Jason, no matter what tangible item he would give him.

When Frank went upstairs a couple minutes later, there was no more avoiding being alone with Jason. The time spent with Frank had lessened the tension between them. Perhaps it wouldn't be as bad as she'd feared.

She picked up the stockings from the table and started toward the parlor. "I guess it's time to play Santa Claus."

He stopped her with a hand on her arm. "How long have you known Frank cared for Amy?"

"I don't recall exactly." Why did he look worried?

"You. . . wouldn't mind if they courted?"

"I think it would be wonderful. Don't you?"

His grin routed every trace of concern from his face. "I sure do, Mrs. Sterling."

He played with the tiny bow at her neck and she stepped nervously away.

"You were right about Frank, I think," he said. "I was so busy being the boss that it never occurred to me to ask God what He wanted anyone else here to be doing."

He took the woolen stockings she'd been unconsciously playing with, then tugged gently at her hand. "Come with me. I want to give you your gift tonight, too. It's in the parlor."

A shaky laugh tripped out at the eagerness in his face. "You're like a child when it comes to Christmas."

He stopped at the archway between the dining room and parlor, where the air was rich with the fragrance of pine. "Stay right here and close your eyes."

She started to protest then subsided. "Yes, sir."

She heard the straw crunch beneath the carpet as he crossed the room, and smelled the sulfur of a lit match, the kerosene of a lamp before he said, "Open your eyes."

He was standing beside the hanging lamp with its large rose-colored shade. The lamp's light illuminated the two paintings in their oval, tortoiseshell frames over the green velvet settee.

Her hand flew to her throat. *Two* paintings. Beside the painting of his parents was a painting of *her* parents.

She walked toward it slowly, stopping at the settee. "It's perfect. How. . . when. . ."

He slipped behind her and slid his arms around her waist. "Amy Henderson painted it for me, copied from your brother's picture of your parents on their wedding day. I asked Amy to do it the night of the play. It seems only right that your parents' picture should hang beside my parents' picture. After all, our families are joined forever by our marriage."

Forever. The word brought back Boston's words from their wedding day—a lifetime is a long time to be unhappy. Had she sentenced Jason to a lifetime of unhappiness?

She shivered as his lips touched the side of her neck softly. "Merry Christmas, Mrs. Sterling."

At his husky whisper, longing and terror joined forces to spiral through her. What was happening between them tonight? She freed herself from his arms and moved to the opposite side of the round marble-topped table in the middle of the room. At least now there would be something between them, and perhaps she could keep her mind clear.

"Jason, I'm sorry." Her fingers twisted the turquoise bow at her waist. "I should never have married you. I meant to make your life easier; instead I only brought you pain."

"Pain?" A frown emphasized the lines the wind and sun had already worked into his young skin. "You've filled my home with cheerfulness and hope. If it weren't for you, Maggie would still be frightened of me, Grace would still be having nightmares, and Frank would still be drinking and gambling and running away from God. How can you possibly think you've hurt me?"

"Tonight at church. . ." It was so degrading to put it into words. She tried to swallow the lump in her throat. She tried again. "I was looking for you. I overheard Miranda tell you . . . tell you. . ."

Even in the mellow lamplight his face looked suddenly pale. His hands fell to his sides in fists. "I'd give everything I own if you hadn't heard that."

She ran the tip of her tongue over her lips, which felt as parched as if she'd spent a week on the desert. "If I hadn't agreed to marry you, you'd be free to marry Miranda now."

His lips narrowed into a line as taut as a bow string. His voice was just as taut. "I don't want to marry Miranda."

"Don't! Don't lie to me. You've never made any secret of your love for her."

He rubbed a hand over his mouth. "How much of my conversation with Miranda did you hear?"

She lowered herself onto the edge of the settee cushion. "Enough to know she claims she still loves you, and would marry you if. . . if. . . ."

Jason sat down beside her and took her hands in a gentle hold that refused to allow her to pull them back. "Did you hear my answer?"

She turned her gaze to the ornate parlor stove, watching

the firelight through the isinglass. "I didn't need to. I know you'd never break your marriage vows, regardless of your love for her."

"Thank God you have that much faith in me, anyway."

She caught her bottom lip between her teeth at his fervent words. Didn't he know she would never believe he could do anything dishonorable?

"The boy I was loved the girl who was Miranda. The man I've become doesn't love the woman Miranda has become." He paused and she fought the temptation to look at him. "It shames me to think I could ever have cared for a woman who has such little regard for another's marriage vows made before God that she'd. . . ."

Her gasp at his suddenly tightened hold stopped his words. He touched his lips to her hands in apology before taking a ragged breath and continuing.

"When I asked you to marry me, I told you I needed you. It was true but not because I needed a housekeeper. I needed you because my house and heart were empty without you. I needed you because I'd fallen in love with you."

Her heart trembled within her, not daring to believe what he was saying.

He trapped the gaze that darted to his.

"I thought if we lived together in a friendly marriage, you might grow to love me. I would never force my. . . my affections. . . on you but I think it's only fair to let you know where I stand. I've been praying for your love. And I give you fair warning that from this moment on, I intend to court my wife good and hard."

It was the tremor in his voice that gave him away. *Why, he was scared stiff!* As frightened as she'd been of not having love returned. The knowledge loosened her throat. "I'm afraid your courting shall prove exceedingly short."

Disappointment dropped over his face like a mask. "I see."

He stood. "I guess. . . ."

"Because," she interrupted with a tiny smile, "your wife has always loved you."

The glory in his face as he pulled her into his arms humbled her. "You dear!" His whisper was rough with love.

Joy shimmered through her. *What a lovely Christmas gift!* And to think that after all the months of trusting God for her husband's love, she almost hadn't recognized the fulfillment of her hope when it came.

His hands slipped up to cradle her face. It seemed to her he studied every inch of it before he slowly lowered his lips to touch hers in a kiss so tender that her heart ached.

Resting his chin against her hair, his arms wrapped around her. "It's quite a life I've tied you to, a hard life with a ready-made family—at least until Frank's ready to take over the farm."

"I'm not complaining."

She shivered as he drew his thumb lightly over her cheek and along her jawline. "No, you never have complained."

"If we love each other and the Lord, we can handle any-thing. Love 'beareth all things, believeth all things, hopeth all things, endureth all things.'"

He kissed her lightly. "Love 'never faileth,'" he whispered. His golden brown eyes filled with promises.

"Never." A smile tugged at her lips. "Or as Grace would say, 'you can't ever change your mind.'"

His chuckle was lost in her kiss.

A Letter To Our Readers

Dear Reader:

In order that we might better contribute to your reading enjoyment, we would appreciate your taking a few minutes to respond to the following questions. When completed, please return to the following:

Rebecca Germany, Editor
Heartsong Presents
P.O. Box 719
Uhrichsville, Ohio 44683

1. Did you enjoy reading *Love's Shining Hope*?
   ❑ Very much. I would like to see more books
      by this author!
   ❑ Moderately
      I would have enjoyed it more if _____

   _____

2. Are you a member of *Heartsong Presents*? Yes   No
   If no, where did you purchase this book? _____

   _____

3. What influenced your decision to purchase this
   book? (Check those that apply.)

   ❑ Cover   ❑ Back cover copy

   ❑ Title   ❑ Friends

   ❑ Publicity   ❑ Other _____

4. On a scale from 1 (poor) to 10 (superior), please rate the following elements.

___Heroine   ___Plot

___Hero   ___Inspirational theme

___Setting   ___Secondary characters

5. What settings would you like to see covered in *Heartsong Presents* books?

_____

_____

6. What are some inspirational themes you would like to see treated in future books?_____

_____

_____

7. Would you be interested in reading other *Heartsong Presents* titles?   ❑ Yes   ❑ No

8. Please check your age range:
❑ Under 18   ❑ 18-24   ❑ 25-34
❑ 35-45   ❑ 46-55   ❑ Over 55

9. How many hours per week do you read? _____

Name _____

Occupation _____

Address _____

City _____ State _____ Zip _____

JoAnn A. Grote

Historical Trilogy

___*The Sure Promise*—Haunted by her own lonely childhood, Laurina Dalen is determined to provide a home for the Wells children. Matthew Strong is determined to meet the medical needs of the prairie dwellers. Laurina and Matthew belong to the praire. . .but first they must belong to each other. HP36 $2.95

___*The Unfolding Heart*—As Millicent and Adam's attraction for each other grows, Millicent realizes she could never make a good wife for a minister. And even if she could, how could she ever bring herself to live with him amid the crudeness and danger of the frontier? HP51 $2.95

___*Treasure of the Heart*—John Wells leaves his fiancée in Minnesota to go in search of the reason for his father's murder. Among the Black Hills of South Dakota he finds the answers he needs, as well as a rare treasure of the heart, Jewell Emerson. HP55 $2.95

···Hearts ♥ng···

Any 12 *Heartsong Presents* titles for only $26.95 *

HISTORICAL ROMANCE IS CHEAPER BY THE DOZEN!

Buy any assortment of twelve *Heartsong Presents* titles and save 25% off of the already discounted price of $2.95 each!

*plus $1.00 shipping and handling per order and sales tax where applicable.

HEARTSONG PRESENTS TITLES AVAILABLE NOW:

__HP 1 A TORCH FOR TRINITY, *Colleen L. Reece*
__HP 2 WILDFLOWER HARVEST, *Colleen L. Reece*
__HP 7 CANDLESHINE, *Colleen L. Reece*
__HP 8 DESERT ROSE, *Colleen L. Reece*
__HP11 RIVER OF FIRE, *Jacquelyn Cook*
__HP12 COTTONWOOD DREAMS, *Norene Morris*
__HP15 WHISPERS ON THE WIND, *Maryn Langer*
__HP16 SILENCE IN THE SAGE, *Colleen L. Reece*
__HP19 A PLACE TO BELONG, *Janelle Jamison*
__HP20 SHORES OF PROMISE, *Kate Blackwell*
__HP23 GONE WEST, *Kathleen Karr*
__HP24 WHISPERS IN THE WILDERNESS, *Colleen L. Reece*
__HP27 BEYOND THE SEARCHING RIVER, *Jacquelyn Cook*
__HP28 DAKOTA DAWN, *Lauraine Snelling*
__HP31 DREAM SPINNER, *Sally Laity*
__HP32 THE PROMISED LAND, *Kathleen Karr*
__HP35 WHEN COMES THE DAWN, *Brenda Bancroft*
__HP36 THE SURE PROMISE, *JoAnn A. Grote*
__HP39 RAINBOW HARVEST, *Norene Morris*
__HP40 PERFECT LOVE, *Janelle Jamison*
__HP43 VEILED JOY, *Colleen L. Reece*
__HP44 DAKOTA DREAM, *Lauraine Snelling*
__HP47 TENDER JOURNEYS, *Janelle Jamison*
__HP48 SHORES OF DELIVERANCE, *Kate Blackwell*
__HP51 THE UNFOLDING HEART, *JoAnn A. Grote*
__HP52 TAPESTRY OF TAMAR, *Colleen L. Reece*
__HP55 TREASURE OF THE HEART, *JoAnn A. Grote*
__HP56 A LIGHT IN THE WINDOW, *Janelle Jamison*
__HP59 EYES OF THE HEART, *Maryn Langer*

(If ordering from this page, please remember to include it with the order form.)

...... Presents ......

Great Inspirational Romance at a Great Price!

Heartsong Presents books are inspirational romances in contemporary and historical settings, designed to give you an enjoyable, spirit-lifting reading experience. You can choose from 104 wonderfully written titles from some of today's best authors like Colleen L. Reece, Brenda Bancroft, Janelle Jamison, and many others.

When ordering quantities less than twelve, above titles are $2.95 each.

SEND TO: Heartsong Presents Reader's Service
P.O. Box 719, Uhrichsville, Ohio 44683

Please send me the items checked above. I am enclosing $_____.
(please add $1.00 to cover postage per order. OH add 6.25% tax. NJ
add 6%.). Send check or money order, no cash or C.O.D.s, please.
To place a credit card order, call 1-800-847-8270.

NAME _____

ADDRESS _____

CITY/STATE_____ ZIP _____

HPS DECEMBER

Heartsong Presents
Love Stories Are Rated G!

That's for godly, gratifying, and of course, great! If you love a thrilling love story, but don't appreciate the sordidness of popular paperback romances, **Heartsong Presents** is for you. In fact, **Heartsong Presents** is the *only inspirational romance book club*, the only one featuring love stories where Christian faith is the primary ingredient in a marriage relationship.

Sign up today to receive your first set of four, never before published Christian romances. Send no money now; you will receive a bill with the first shipment. You may cancel at any time without obligation, and if you aren't completely satisfied with any selection, you may return the books for an immediate refund!

Imagine. . .four new romances every month—two historical, two contemporary—with men and women like you who long to meet the one God has chosen as the love of their lives. . .all for the low price of $9.97 postpaid.

To join, simply complete the coupon below and mail to the address provided. **Heartsong Presents** romances are rated G for another reason: They'll arrive *Godspeed!*